aftershock

ALSO BY KELLY EASTON

THE LIFE HISTORY OF A STAR

WALKING ON AIR

MARGARET K. MCELDERRY BOOKS

kelly easton

aftershock

MARGARET K. MCELDERRY BOOKS
NEW YORK — LONDON — TORONTO — SYDNEY

Margaret K. McElderry Books
An imprint of Simon & Schuster Children's
Publishing Division
1230 Avenue of the Americas
New York, New York 10020
Book design by Krista Vossen
The text for this book is set in Minion.
Manufactured in the United States of America
10 9 8 7 6 5 4 3 2 1
Library of Congress Cataloging-in-Publication
Data
Easton, Kelly.
Aftershock / Kelly Easton.—1st ed.
p. cm.
Summary: In shock and unable to speak after
being in a car accident in Oregon which has
killed his parents, seventeen-year-old Adam
journeys across the country to his home in
Rhode Island.
ISBN-13: 978-1-4169-0052-8
ISBN-10: 1-4169-0052-7 (hardcover)
[1. Grief—Fiction. 2. Voyages and travels—
Fiction. 3. Traffic accidents—Fiction.] I. Title.
PZ7.E13155Def 2006
[Fic]—dc22
2005028403

How many roads must a man walk down
Before you can call him a man . . .
—Bob Dylan

FOR MICHAEL RUBEN

And to some other fine boys and men:
Isaac Easton Spivack, Gordon Easton, Michael Easton,
Robert Easton, Erik Mills, and Herb Ruben.

Thank you to Charlotte Ruben for
proofreading for me. And many thanks to
Karen Wojtyla, Sarah Payne, and Emma D. Dryden of
Margaret K. McElderry Books.

∧∧∧

Definitions from *The Oxford American Dictionary* and *The American
Heritage Dictionary of the English Language*

www.kellyeaston.com

aftershock

kelly easton

CHAPTER 1

truncate:
to shorten by cutting off a part; to cut short.

It was dark the way a shadow is dark, the light shrinking around it, spreading night like a puddle. The girl with the black bra kept popping into my mind. The way her breasts jiggled when she shook her fist at the cops. How she kicked the fat one when he tried to yank her off the podium.

The girl wasn't even pretty. She had hair like bleached straw, and tanned leather skin. She looked like she belonged on the back of a Harley.

But that black bra—her breasts. When she ripped off her shirt and swung it around her head, the entire crowd stopped breathing.

I tried to think of something else, something that would help me, us, like how long we had been driving through the woods, how far since the last town, when it was that I'd last seen another car. But I couldn't get a grip on my mind. It kept jumping backward to the antiwar rally in Seattle, the girl, her bra.

My parents were dead. That much I knew. Sprawled out across each other like teenagers on some lovers' lane.

I wasn't sure how long I'd been standing outside the car, didn't remember unbuckling my seat belt. (*They* hadn't been wearing them.)

We were leaving "Hicksville"—as Dad called Idaho—heading east toward Bristol, Rhode Island, our home. The only radio stations we could get were country. "Crazy," by Patsy Cline, was floating from the speakers.

My mom was saying how the strip of sunset looked like a thread of blood across the sky. Wouldn't my English teacher, Ms. Ross, enjoy that? The irony? That only a minute after Mom said that, her voice gentle and awed, she herself would have a thread of blood from her eye to her mouth. And nothing else. Nothing visible to explain her lack of pulse or the way her eyes had gone marble, like she was sleepwalking in cold dreams.

Internal injuries. The two words came into my head like a pop-up on a computer screen.

"Who do you love most?" my parents would joke when I was little.

"I bought you that skateboard," Dad would coax.

"I love Dad more," I'd answer.

"I took you to the museum," Mom would counter.

"Mom, then."

"I read to you all the time," Dad would grin. He had the most amazing buckteeth. He couldn't even keep his lips closed over them. It made him look like he was always smiling.

"So does Mom."

"I threw up for nine months so you could live!" Mom saved the trump card for last.

And it was my mom I leaped for. I didn't even think about it. My fingers groped for a pulse at her wrist, her neck. My ear pressed to her chest.

It was her I went for first.

She was wearing Dad's denim shirt, the sleeves rolled up, her wrists as thin as birch twigs. In her hand, still, was my language journal with the definitions. It was one of the things I was doing to make up for missing school. She'd been creating funny sentences using the words. "The sunset is *elongated,*" she'd said, "like a thread of blood across the sky."

I shook her. Nothing. I lifted her head, then laid it gently back onto the seat.

And I thought, okay, maybe I'm dead too. That's why the planet is tilting, why I don't have any air in my lungs, why my body feels like it's been shot with Novocain. I'm not laid out like her, but there might be different ways of being dead.

Like there are different ways of believing in God. I was my own dead. She was hers.

"Dad," I said. My voice was absolutely calm. Just "Dad," like I was asking for ten bucks to go to the movies.

It was the last word I would say for months.

CHAPTER 2

fortitude:
courage in bearing pain or trouble.

The locker room at my school smells like pee. About ten years back, a couple of jocks with a complex had a contest to see who could piss the farthest. They stood with their backs against the lockers and aimed for the showers.

Their names were Derek Gut and Gary Reamer. With names like that, you could see why they had a problem.

I don't remember who won the contest, but what I do know is that neither of them made it to where the water could have washed away the evidence. Their pee landed about halfway, right on the floor that leads from the lockers to the showers.

The contest became a tradition, a ritual. I had to do it myself. And my aim, my distance, was about as bad as theirs.

When you're a guy you have to act like an asshole sometimes, so that the real assholes won't bug you. I've always wanted to teach that to the three or four kids who don't get it and spend their lives being the butt of the joke.

The family business has kept me busy enough to miss a lot of dumb stuff, like the time Jacks, Bud, and Cory tried to jump their cars from Cork's Ridge to the other side. Jacks and Cory made it; they had fast cars. But Bud's gray Toyota took a nosedive and got wedged beneath the precipice. I'd had inventory that night, so I had a decent excuse not to endanger my life. And if I remember right, I even tried to talk them out of it. Not that I could have. Bud had to be rescued by a helicopter. But he made it. At least he made it out.

Still, I've done a lot of other stupid stuff with the guys. Like Valentine's Day my sophomore year. Cory got the bright idea about raiding the girls' locker room. "They'll be wearing little red undies with hearts and shit," he said.

So, at the end of PE, instead of showering, we snuck in. There were about ten of us guys, and we hunched on the benches behind the lockers, waiting. The girls came streaming in, sweaty from the basketball court. I don't know what we expected—that they would walk in naked? It was so dumb. Within two seconds they saw us and started screaming their heads off.

Except Mira Winstett. Mira walked to her locker, opened it, and started to take off her gym clothes.

I didn't know Mira then. I'd watched her, seen her move down the hall with her headphones on like she was in some kind of a trance. I'd sat next to her in geometry. When she bent over a problem, her hair fell over her face like a threshold to another country. I remember thinking that. And that the country was exotic and I would never have a passport.

That day, Mira stepped over the boys as if we didn't exist. She pulled her clothes from the locker and laid them out. Most of the girls wore T-shirts to gym, but Mira was wearing a long-sleeved white blouse. I realized, in that moment, that she always wore long sleeves. As many times as I'd looked at her, I'd never seen her arms.

Mira took off her shoes and socks, and started to unbutton her blouse. She was at the bottom button when a couple of girls broke the new silence and squealed. Girls who had never spoken to Mira in their lives rushed forward to save her from the indignity of the boys' bugging eyes, what Ms. Ross would later call "the male gaze."

Amy Harver, the head coach, came dashing in. As soon as she saw us, *she* started yelling. Harver was much more articulate than the girls. The words "little perverts" figured into her accusations prominently.

We were marched back to the boys' locker room, and that was when it struck me the most, the stench of pee, the outcome of years of boys missing the shower. The girls' locker room smelled like talc, roses, lilac, and deodorant. The boys' smelled like a sewer.

Maybe that's why the black-bra girl kept popping into my mind. It reminded me of that time with Mira. That last button she undid before she was tackled by the girls.

$$\mathcal{MW}$$

"Dad," I said. Not for a second did it occur to me that he might also be dead. That *both* of them could die at the same time.

There was no answer. I pulled my eyes from my mom.

Dad was leaning forward against the steering wheel. That's what I thought. Leaning. The word "slumped" didn't come to my mind. I couldn't have dealt with that word.

I ran around to the driver-side door, opened it, and yanked him back from the steering wheel.

And that's when I knew that I wasn't just drifting in my own dead apart from theirs. The right side of his face was smashed and pulpy. A patch of skin was peeled back from his cheek. His eye seemed about to come out. A bunch of his teeth, his awesome buckteeth, were stuck in the steering wheel. It looked like a bad makeup job in a horror flick. I looked at my dad's face and I pissed my pants. My mind flashed to the locker room.

And I knew I was alive.

CHAPTER 3

fugue:
1. a musical composition with several themes, which gradually builds to a complex form, with marked climax at the end. 2. a period during which a person suffers from loss of memory.

Mira's popularity soared in the few weeks after she almost took off her clothes. The girls tugged on her sleeve, whispered and giggled. The boys offered her high fives. Someone wrote across the lockers: *Mira is a Babe.* She would later call it "my horrible fifteen minutes of fame."

For our little trick in the locker room, the ten of us were suspended from school for three days, then treated to a series of lectures by a lady from the Rape Prevention Center, plus one from Ms. Ross on feminist theory.

It was a very big deal.

I stood outside the car for a long time. The darkness moved over me. No more edges or corners. Just black sky. Rain started. The sound of the drops reminded me of another background noise I'd been listening to all along: the sound of panting. Only then did I remember the deer.

I found it in the ditch a few hundred feet away. It was if some considerate person had laid it there to avoid traffic.

The deer was like my mom, nothing wrong with it that I could see, just its back leg splayed, its tongue vibrating from its breath.

I should shoot it, I thought, *put it out of its misery*—but I didn't have a gun. My parents were pacifists. We'd driven all the way from Rhode Island to Seattle to be in a peace vigil that had turned violent: black-bra girl shrieking obscenities, students turning over cars and swinging their signs at the cops, a fire set in a trash can.

We'd been to tons of peace vigils in New England: people singing folk songs, holding hands, making speeches. We'd never experienced anything like this.

"It's like something you'd expect after a football game," Dad said.

"Human beings are so depressing." My mom shook her head. And we left.

"Well, at least we're having a little vacation," Dad offered.

"A little?" Mom joked. "We still have to drive across the country." We'd had a great time getting there, but I could tell she wanted to get home.

I opened the back door of the car. I didn't know what I was looking for: something to help the deer. My backpack had spilled open. A couple of books, my wallet, a bottle of water, and my Swiss Army knife were on the floor. I left it all. On the seat next to mine was our picket sign from the rally, which quoted Mark Twain: MAN IS THE ONLY ANIMAL THAT BLUSHES. OR NEEDS TO. I thought it was a pretty vague sign, but Dad had come up with it, and Mom was thrilled.

Then I noticed something strange: My dad's body had fallen onto my mom's, their arms now touching, their hair mixed together. I don't know how gravity pulled him to her like that—the car was completely level—but it was right, their being together like that. It was right.

I went back to the deer.

Its breath was slower. Its eyelids were fluttering.

As I watched the deer die, the weirdest things kept popping into my mind. Things that didn't have to do with anything. Like I thought about this psychotic squirrel that lived in our yard at home. Sometimes when I was outside, the squirrel would run up my body like I was a tree. My mom thought it was the funniest thing in the world. "You should've seen your face . . ." She would double over with laughter. "A blind squirrel."

"Yeah, very funny," I'd retort.

And I thought about the sign on my parents' bookstore

that said CLOSED, with a peace sign in the O. I thought of Mira: how torn her jeans were when she came into the bookstore, and how I didn't find out until months later that she had come in there not for *The Collected Works of Camus,* but for me. I thought of my aunt's autistic kid, Joey, who would jump to one side if you came near him, as if you were fire and him paper, and I thought of Ms. Ross singing "I Am Woman" at the end of her feminist lecture. She sang it so well that instead of laughing at her, we all broke into applause.

The deer stopped breathing. I don't know why I felt I had to wait and watch it die, like some kind of a witness. But I did.

I went back to the car. The front end was completely smashed.

The night was silent, the trees looming, complicit. I put both hands on the car and closed my eyes. It is so hard to explain it now. It was like I was leaving my life there to be taken, but no one wanted to have it.

I tried to bring a word into my mouth, to unwrap a prayer from my tongue and give voice to it.

I opened my mouth to my own soundlessness.

The road went off in a straight line through the trees as far as I could see, then shrank away in the distance.

Two weeks earlier, I'd sat in Art History while Dr. Weissman went on about De Chirico's paintings, the way the trains he inserted in them torqued the perspective.

The pines all around me quivered in the damp air.

I started walking.

CHAPTER 4

recalcitrant:
resisting authority or control.

My parents had wanted a big family. "A bunch of kids eating granola and writing on the walls" is how my mom put it. "Enough to make one of those family rock bands," my dad added.

But something happened to my mom. Doctors said she had a growth.

This whole conversation took place when I was about thirteen. We'd been camping at Fort Getty in Jamestown, and we were taking the ferry to Newport. Narragansett Bay was full of sailboats with colored sails. The water was bright blue. It was one of those times when you forget the endless days of frozen winter and New England shines and you know you could never bear to leave it.

My mom was the type who would tell anyone anything. She didn't have a filter. She wasn't the least bit self-conscious. "The doctors told me I had a growth," she explained, "and I pictured some kind of shrub taking

14

root in my body. A chubby evergreen. A winding vine."

"It was one of the few times when we *didn't* question authority," Dad added.

"The doctors drove through me like a train. They put a tunnel in me, and I was too scared to say anything."

It had never bothered me that I was an only child. It was like the three of us were siblings. We ran the bookstore, did yoga together, watched the news fanatically, played board games all winter, and gardened in the spring. My dad and I surfed. "Your parents are the coolest people I've ever met," Mira told me the first time she came to dinner.

But as I walked on the road, it flashed in my mind that I needed someone to look after, someone to pull myself together for: a little sister, twin brothers, a baby to hold in my arms and protect, someone to keep me moving.

I searched my mind for family members. My dad's parents lived in Guam, where my grandfather did some kind of navy work. I hadn't seen them in years. My mom's parents had died within a year of each other when she was in college, both of cancer. All I could think of was my mom's sister, Margarite, and her autistic son, Joey. Margarite was my mom's opposite. My mom was blond and fair-skinned. Margarite had black hair and darker skin. My mom was soft-spoken. Margarite was loud and forceful. She also swore like a sailor.

The rain stopped, but my clothes were wet. I had been

walking so long that my legs could barely move. My feet were swollen and blistered in my high-tops. I could feel blood flowing down the back of my heel. A couple of cars had passed. I had tried to stop one of them. When the second one went by, with a blast of country music and a screech of tires, I didn't even bother to look up.

I kept getting reminders of my aliveness: the pain, the thirst carving a dry ravine through my throat, the chill in my bones. I resisted the urge to lie down and sleep in the middle of the road, to pour myself out like pancake batter on a grill, be run over, and get it over with.

I came up with tricks to keep myself moving. For a while I pretended the moon was Mira's face in the sky, and I only had to keep walking to reach it.

I imagined that Joey was with me and I had to get him home. I remembered the time he and my aunt Margarite came to visit us after her husband left her.

He had been in the military. They were living in Hawaii. As soon as Joey was diagnosed as being profoundly autistic, her husband ran off from both the military and her, disappeared while on a quick jaunt to Thailand, leaving behind only a brief note: *Can't deal with this. Found someone who suits my dreams.*

"'Suits my dreams'?" Margarite howled at our kitchen table. "What the hell is that supposed to mean? Who gives a shit about his dreams?"

I was ten. It was my job to follow Joey around, to make

sure he didn't get into trouble while my mom and dad and Margarite drank daiquiris and commiserated about the end of her marriage. "That son of a bitch," she swore. "Ten minutes after he leaves me, he remarries. Now his new wife is pregnant. I hope she gives birth to Siamese twins."

"Oh, Margarite." My mom stroked her hair. "You've got to release all this anger."

"Anger is energy. It's good fucking energy."

"You've got a point," my dad agreed. He used to be a boxer, so he knew about that kind of energy. "It can be creative. Productive."

Margarite beamed at him.

"Nonsense," Mom said. She never got it, the way some people feel stirred up inside, like there's a storm in their chest, a tornado in their gut, and they have to find a way to release it. She never got violence.

It was easy to look after Joey. His only interest in life was putting things in a row. Our house was pretty chaotic: stacks of books, coffee mugs—occasionally with some specimen growing in them—paperweights, magazines, about ten years' worth of Amnesty International pamphlets.

My parents were really into Amnesty. It's an organization that researches human-rights violations throughout the world and advocates for the victims. Still, I doubt they ever read all those pamphlets. But it was like they thought that if they threw them away, they were neglecting the women who would be stoned to death for adultery, the

Chinese dissidents who were being tortured, the Colombian journalists who had disappeared, the Rwandans who were being murdered, the Asian children who were being kidnapped and put into prostitution.

Joey worked methodically. He grabbed the stack of pamphlets and lined them up from one wall to the other.

Next, he went for hard objects: paperweights, stones. He seemed to have a system for categorizing things. He included the coffee cups, for example, but not the vases. The spacing between the objects appeared to be mathematically exact. Later, when I brought Joey in and reported his progress, Margarite said, "Yeah, he's a frigging genius when it comes to spacing."

"You and Joey will come live with us," Mom was saying. "It's as simple as that."

Dad's face went white, but he nodded his head as if he agreed.

Margarite collapsed facedown on the table and sobbed. "You can't take us on. No one can."

"Maybe the daiquiris were a bad idea," Dad said.

Joey had no response to his mom's emotion. He rocked back and forth on his heels and gazed at a spot on the wall as if something secret were written there.

"Things will get better, Margarite." Mom stroked her sister's hair. "They can only get better. I promise."

"That only happens for *you*," Margarite said.

The sky seemed to be lightening. I wondered if I was imagining it. Could I have been walking all night?

I tripped on a branch in the road and sprawled out, my hands skinned and bloodied like a kid's. I lay there for a few minutes, my limbs like water. But then I heard something coming from the woods. Voices. Singing. The soft tones, the obscure language, made me think of how angels might sound if they put music to their prayers.

I sat up and looked. A faint light bounced off the trees. I dragged myself to my feet and stumbled into the woods.

In a clearing, surrounded by a circle of small flames, was a group of angels. They were all women, and they were wingless, but they wore white gowns, and they moved in a circle like children chanting nursery rhymes.

I went toward them, thinking in some way that I might join them, even though I was male. I would join them, flicker through the trees, be recreated as light.

One of the angels coughed. An angel choking on her prayer, I thought. Another howled like a wolf.

I stumbled forward, my legs faltering, breaking through where Coughing Angel had let go of a hand in order to cover her mouth. Then I fell, face down, into the center of the circle of their prayers.

CHAPTER 5

conventicle:
a clandestine religious meeting, especially of
nonconformists or dissenters.

The earth was cool and soft. I wondered if I could sink into it all the way. I'm sure it was only a few seconds that I lay there before the angels rushed toward me, but in that time, I flashed on the cocktail napkin that was framed and hung in the entrance of our house. I always looked at it when I came in and hung my baseball cap on the hat rack. In barely legible writing was a poem: *This is the wing, the broken wing. This is the bone grown wrong. Still the wing flaps. The feathers lift. On air as bold as strong.* The poem was my dad's, and it was what brought my parents together.

My mom was in Maine on spring break with some friends. They were in a dive bar having beers, celebrating someone's engagement, oohing and ahhing over her ring.

My mom was kind of bored. "I was twenty years old," she told me, "and I felt like an impostor with those girls.

None of the things that excited them excited me, like clothes or hairstyles or frat parties."

To avoid having to express a bunch of phony emotion, she offered to get the next round of beers.

My dad worked construction during the day. At night he was pursuing a career as a boxer. He'd finished a fight an hour earlier, and he'd been whipped. His eye was swollen shut, his lip split, his muscles bruised. He realized that whatever it took to really succeed as a fighter, he didn't have it. So he was bummed out, sitting at the bar by himself, scrawling poetry on the cocktail napkin.

My mom came to the bar. "Hey, blondie," some guy shouted at her. "Wanna join my club?" My mom gave him the finger. She turned away and noticed a "big thug" with a swollen eye and bruises all over his face. *What a classy place,* she thought, but then she saw that he was writing, scrawling words with the nub of a pencil onto a cocktail napkin. If there was one thing my mom was nuts about, it was writing. She had to read everything: books, newspapers, magazines, even notices that were hanging in supermarket windows.

She sidled up next to him and lifted his arm a bit to peer down at what he was writing. Too tired to be interested, he ignored her.

This is the wing, the broken wing. This is the bone grown wrong, she read.

"You wrote that?" she asked.

"Uh-huh."

As she explained it to me: "I looked at this big tall guy with the black eye and blood on his shirt, and then I read his beautiful words, and I knew it. That he was the person I was meant to be with." She never brought the drinks to her friends.

I opened my eyes. I was surrounded by angels. Some were kneeling next to me. A couple of others stood back as though they didn't like what they saw.

Hands were on me. I was being turned and prodded; their faces were dangling above me like ornaments on a tree. It seems strange, but I felt giddy with joy from their attention.

"Is he hurt?"

"Careful . . ." Their voices surrounded me. "He looks sick." "See if he has a gun." "Do you think he's lost?" "Are you hurt?" "What's your name?"

I looked from face to face. They were of all ages, but mostly older, mostly heavyset—the kind of women who came into the shop and stayed for hours, then walked out with a pile of books on things like herbs and homeopathy and blank journals to record their dreams.

One angel was gorgeous, though. She had long, dark hair and eyes like the deer, wide and startled. "He looks like Prince William, doesn't he?" she said.

"Who?"

"You know, the England guy, the future king. Princess Di's son."

"Ohhh. Him."

"Kind of," another offered.

"Prince William with buckteeth." Coughing Angel chuckled.

"You shouldn't be out here with that cold," Howling Angel scolded.

"It's getting light. What will we do with him?"

"Hospital?"

"Do you want to go to the hospital?" Coughing Angel asked.

I shook my head, and struggled to sit up, to show them I was okay, that I was just resting.

"Who are you?"

"Did you tie one on?"

"What's your name?"

"I think you're cute, whoever you are," Pretty Angel said.

"Come on," Coughing Angel coaxed. "Tell us what you're doing in the woods. Were you spying?"

I'd walked all night, my mind fairly clear, trying to figure out what I should do, how I should find help.

I knew that what I needed to do was tell them about the road, the car, the miles I'd walked. Time and space. Distance. But the fact of the accident, my parents' death, kept skirting the periphery of my mind, like an answer you know you know on a test, but you can't quite remember.

A gunshot sounded. Howling Angel howled, and someone told her to shut up. The candles were blown out.

"Let's go, Prince William." Pretty Angel pulled me to my feet. "The hunters have arrived. They'll shoot anything that moves."

CHAPTER 6

serendipity:
the making of pleasant discoveries by accident,
the knack of doing this.

Aunt Margarite never did move in with us. Instead, she wandered the country, finally settling in Florida, where she opened up a shop that did import-export. She and Joey traveled to Mexico, Central America, Africa, India, and China; they brought back Guatemalan blankets, wooden elephants, prayer shawls, and exotic art. Every now and then she'd call my mom and tell her she'd met *the one*. The first was a Cuban man who ran a cigar shop in Miami Beach. The second was a reggae singer from Jamaica. The third was a traffic cop. Then my mom wouldn't hear from her again until disaster struck. "This one stole a hundred dollars from her and went back to his wife and kids in Texas," Mom would report. "That guy from New York said she had to institutionalize Joey if she wanted him to stay."

My mom fretted and worried about her sister con- stantly. "It's always been that way for Margarite. Everything

came easily to me. But she's dyslexic. She flunked a grade
and got in trouble constantly. She has an uncanny knack for
choosing losers. And Joey. I wish there was something I
could do to make it better."

They were half sisters. Margarite's dad was a railway
worker who stayed on a train one day and never came back.
Mom's dad was an English teacher.

"You do all you can," Dad said. "It's out of your control."

But my mom always wanted to take care of her,
although Margarite was four years older. Mom couldn't
stand for anyone to suffer. If there was a stray dog, she'd
take it in and put a photo up in the shop until someone
adopted it. If there was a sick neighbor, or a death in someone's family, she'd be there with one of her barely edible
vegetarian concoctions. There were people who came into
the bookstore just to talk, to tell her about their knee surgery or latest romance, and she listened. She listened to
them all.

I woke up knowing three things: that I was in a bed, that I
was clean, and that I was naked. The rest of my mind was
blank.

I looked around the room. It was a motel room, with
just a bed, a dresser, a hot plate, and a TV nailed to a stand,
but the walls were decorated as if someone had been there
for a while: photographs of celebrities cut out from magazines, a calendar with a cocker spaniel on it, a couple of

drawings of fairies. Next to me, thumbtacked to the wall, were two tarot cards, a cartoon, and some fortunes. The cartoon was of a waitress taking an order; she pulls a tampon from behind her ear. "What's this tampon doing behind my ear—and where's my pencil?" the caption said. The fortunes were more promising: YOUR LUCK IS ABOUT TO CHANGE; YOUR TALENTS WILL SOON BE RECOGNIZED; YOU ARE A FRIEND TO ANIMALS. It was only later that I'd see the humor in that one, how it related to myself, a wild man found in the woods.

My clothes weren't anywhere in sight.

"You're awake." Pretty Angel appeared. She was wearing a uniform, a gray polyester dress with a soiled white apron. Her hair was in a hairnet. "I didn't know if you'd still be here when I got back. I even worried that you'd steal all my stuff and hit the road—not that there's much to steal. I washed your clothes, but I don't have a dryer. They're hanging in the bathroom. What's your name? Hmmm? Me, Stacey. You?" She took the apron off and flung it on the floor. "I'll just have to call you William, then." Stacey walked into the bathroom. A second later, I heard water running. "Boy, you really passed out. What happened to you?" She came back out and took her hair down in front of the mirror. "I used to like eggs. You know? There was a year when I was even on the egg diet. I ate every kind of omelet you could dream of: jam omelets, tomato omelets, green-chili omelets, marshmallow omelets. I lost, like, eight pounds in a month. Of course, you could only use the whites, but that was okay. The yolks remind me of chicks anyway, you know the little chicks that would've been—all, like, fluffy and yellow and cute."

I nodded. *My brain feels like an egg,* I thought: a cracked one, little fragments missing, pieces of shell.

"You know PETA, the People for the Ethical Treatment of Animals? Before I joined the Wiccans I belonged to that. It was an okay organization, but the people were boring. You know, like 'my dog this,' or 'my parrot that.' They were the types who couldn't deal with people, mostly, so they obsessed about animals."

I nodded. My parents had belonged to it for a while.

"There's this other PETA, too. You heard of them? People Eating Tasty Animals. Those are just assholes who took over the name. Anyway, I hate eggs now. All breakfast foods. Even the smell of coffee makes me want to puke. Maybe I could go on disability or something, since diner food makes me so sick. What do you think?"

I shrugged. The word "woods" came to my mind. I wondered if I'd had a stroke.

She went into the bathroom and turned off the water. I could hear the sound of clothes being removed: a zipper, a snap. "I was starving this morning, after chanting all night. Wiccans are cool and everything, but they don't know that a good time should include food and beverage." I heard the sound of splashing water. "Ahh."

I closed my eyes and drifted. *If I could just stay in this bed and sleep for the rest of my life,* I thought, *everything would be fine.*

"Prince William? Are you asleep again?"

I opened my eyes. She was naked under her towel, her skin pink and steaming. Despite everything, my body responded.

"Do you realize how long it's been since I slept?" she said. "About thirty hours. This group is so amazing. I mean, I can feel my energy transforming. It's just they do every-thing in the middle of the damn night. I started hallucinat-ing at work, I swear, after I'd served my fiftieth plate of eggs. I saw men climbing into the yolks. Little lumberjacks. You know the spotted owls? The loggers are destroying their habitat. And to really piss off the environmentalists, they kill the owls and nail them up around town. I hate Idaho. The most famous resident of the state is Mark Fuhrman, that racist cop in the O. J. Simpson trial. He writes books. He lied under oath and got to become a celebrity. Idaho sucks. Land of the potato. Whoop-de-doo."

I wanted to ask her questions, like where she was from, and how old she was, but my voice couldn't make the trip from my throat to my mouth. I nodded to encourage her to keep talking.

"I'm beat. I burned my hand on the grill and kept spilling coffee onto the saucers." She pulled the covers back and looked at me. "I just want to sleep. Okay? No funny business."

I nodded.

She dropped the towel and climbed in next to me. I pulled the covers up over her. She put her head on my chest and I wrapped my arm around her. "Prince William," she sighed, and in a minute, she was snoring.

CHAPTER 7

dissent:
to have or express a different opinion.

Sleep had always been a chore. When I was little, my mom and dad had to read me a million books before I'd nod off, and I pulled all those tricks to stay up longer: asking for a glass of water, saying I was hungry or scared, begging to sleep in their room. Once I was old enough, I'd sneak a flashlight and stay up late reading. If the book was good, I would read the whole thing, then not be able to get up in the morning.

My mom was an early bird, though. I'd hear the radio news—National Public Radio—smell the coffee brewing, feel the heat kick on, and then she'd come padding in. "Come on, buddy, up and at 'em." She'd go out, but five minutes later she'd be back. She was a walking snooze alarm. "Rise and shine. Let's get moving." Then, finally, "Adam, you're going to be late!"

My dad was the same. She had to pry him out of bed

too. I wondered how she got anything done, going back and forth trying to wake us.

But now sleep was a place to fall, to forget. I slept while Stacey went out with her Wiccan friends at night. I slept with her when she came home from work. I dreamed only of the pleasant things. I never dreamed of the accident. I dreamed of the high school, the big white doors swinging open to greet me. Or I dreamed of Mira. In a life that was fairly uneventful and calm—school, sports, the bookstore— Mira rose up as something heightened, exciting.

It was a few weeks after the locker-room episode that Mira came into the bookstore. We have one of those ladders that goes up to the ceiling and slides along the shelves. I was standing at the top of it, stocking some leftover books we had from a signing. The book was by some local guy who lived a life modeled after Thoreau. We hadn't sold many copies.

Mira walked in, and I had the feeling I always did when I saw her: a lump in my throat, thoughts flying out of my brain like birds from a cage.

"Marion the librarian," she said.

"Huh?"

"Seeing you up there reminded me of that scene in *The Music Man*."

"Oh, yeah."

"Did you see that movie? There's this number

where Shirley Jones dances around among the books."

"Uh, I think so."

"It's pretty corny, but I love musicals."

"What are you looking for?" I said.

Later, she told me that if I'd said, "May I help you?" she would have asked for a book, bought it, and left.

"I want to ride on that," she said like a kid.

I thought of Dad's mantra: "No customers on the ladder."

"Sure."

She started climbing up before I had a chance to climb down. I had to squeeze past her, our bodies touching. I have never wanted to freeze time so much in my life.

"Ready?" I asked.

"Uh-huh." She hung on.

I sped her back and forth across the shelves. I hoped my parents wouldn't come back from lunch; I'd be in for it if they did.

The store was completely empty. No customers. Just us. It was one of those rare moments where life hands you what you most want, and you just try to keep your mouth from hanging open and go along with it.

She was wearing ripped-up jeans. As I pushed her, I could see her leg through the holes. Her skin was tan, almost gold. I was dying to touch it.

"Wait! Stop!" she said.

That freaked me out, because it was like she knew what I was thinking. But she had grabbed a book. "I found it!

How can you keep him here? Where no one can reach him?"

"Huh?"

"Camus," she insisted. "I was looking for his *Collected Works*."

"Maybe it's an honor to be high up," I joked.

"Do you know that story where the schoolteacher has to turn the prisoner over to the prison, but instead he gives him his freedom? But it doesn't matter because the guy chooses prison."

"'The Guest.' That's my favorite story."

"Mine, too! And that essay on the guy who pushes the rock up the hill over and over again, but when it rolls down, at least his mind is free."

"Yeah, that's how I feel when I'm reshelving all of these books. Like Sisyphus."

She laughed. "Wow. I can't believe you've read that too. You must learn so much being around all these books."

"Except I don't finish half the books I start."

When she climbed down, I put my hands on her legs to steady her. It was instinctual.

"I *always* finish what I start." When we were at eye level, she stopped. I'm six-one. She's about five feet at most. For her head to be level with mine, she had to be up four rungs on the ladder.

I was starting to sweat. I could feel it on my forehead. "We have a section on existentialism," I said.

She was so close, her breath was on my face. Her hair

smelled like wheat or grass. "Why do you watch me?" she asked.

"Huh?"

"In school, when I pass you in the hall. You always look like you're about to talk to me, but then you don't say anything. You just stare."

Because you're beautiful popped into my head, but I had a feeling I shouldn't say it.

"You wouldn't hear me if I talked to you," I explained. "You've always got headphones on."

"Can you keep a secret?"

"Sure." The fact that my voice kept coming out calmly amazed me. My heart was pounding; my legs felt weak.

"I have those on, sometimes, even without music playing. It's like carving a little space for myself, like a . . . retreat in the midst of quite a lot of bullshit."

I nodded my head like I knew what she was talking about.

"So I don't have to hear about this one did this, and that one did that, and he's mean to her, and she slept with him," she explained.

"That time in the locker room . . . ," I started.

"Everyone asks me about it," she said.

"Sorry."

"I wasn't really going to take off my clothes. No way. I just wanted to show everyone how stupid they were being. But you didn't really answer my question."

"What's that?"

"Why you stare at me?"

"I guess I wonder what you're thinking."

She had the book in one hand. She rested the other on my shoulder. "This is what I'm thinking," she said, and she kissed me.

It wasn't the first time I'd kissed a girl, but it was the first time it really felt like more than what it is, a couple of tongues wobbling around in wet space. Mira's kiss was like a white beam moving through me, lighting up places I didn't know about. I know that sounds corny, but that's what it felt like.

When I put my arms around her, her feet flew off the ladder, but I didn't stop. I just held onto her, held her above the ground. It was one of the most perfect moments of my life.

The bells on the door rang; I heard a customer come in, then quickly exit. New Englanders value privacy.

And I kept kissing her. It felt that natural, that right.

"Wow!" Stacey sat up in the bed. "Unbelievable. No one's ever kissed me like that before. Like . . . with *love*."

I opened my eyes. It was dark, just the bathroom light on, buzzing like a fly. I had no idea where I was. I would eventually get used to it, the blankness that kept coming over me, especially when I woke up. But then, it put me into a complete panic. I wondered if I had gotten drunk at a party and wound up with someone I didn't know.

Stacey flipped on a light. She was smiling, but the look of pleasure on her face melted, the way Mira was melting beneath my fingertips. "Oh, I get it," she said. "It's someone else. Someone from your silent, invisible life." She started crying. "It's not even me."

CHAPTER 8

imbrication:
an arrangement that overlaps like tiles, as the scales
of a fish.

For the most part, Stacey seemed pretty happy to have me there. I was like a pet, maybe: unconditional love, not too much trouble. She worked the morning shift in a diner on the highway. She came back around noon, beat, her apron pockets full of dollar bills and change.

While she was gone, I would clean the place up and make lunch. It was tiny, one of seven rooms in a small motel. The first time I cleaned took me forever, though. The place was filthy, a mushroom actually growing out of a crack in the bathroom floor, the inside of the toilet brown.

After I cleaned, I'd stare out the window at the parking lot or watch CNN. I watched the same headlines over and over. It was like I was looking for something or someone, like *I Spy* or *Where's Waldo?*

Stacey would come in just after noon and go on about all the assholes who came in for breakfast and how she hated having to smile at them and pretend their jokes were funny just so she could get a good tip. She had all these brochures for warm, foreign places. She wanted to apply for a job on a cruise line or Club Med, meet rich people, get a tan.

At first, Stacey asked me a bunch of questions: Why was I in Idaho? What school had I gone to? Was I from another country? Had I been in the war? She shoved a pad at me and gave me a pencil, but writing was like speaking: I couldn't or wouldn't do it. It was like the formations, the structures that offered language to my thoughts, had disappeared.

I didn't have amnesia exactly. Pieces of my life drifted past me like ice floes on water. It was just that things weren't connecting in my brain, as if the messages in the synapses were asteroids and shooting stars going past each other, none of them making it to their destination.

One day, Stacey came home a bit early. "I had the worst day," she complained. "This guy came in, and every time I walked by, he nagged me for a refill. His kidneys are probably going to fail within six months. He hogs my table for like two hours, then takes off without leaving me so much as a dime. Nothing!"

Usually, I got up as soon as she came home. But I'd been watching this show about Iraq. The perky blond anchorwoman was interviewing an Iraqi woman whose whole family was wiped out *accidentally* by American soldiers. A lawyer was suing the government on her behalf, although American military law prohibited it. "What is this like? I mean, how are you managing to cope with the loss of your daughters, your husband, your uncle?" the anchor asked.

"I am *not*," the Iraqi woman said slowly, emphasizing the last word so it sounded like she was saying she didn't exist any more, rather than she wasn't coping. It was clear the woman had nothing more to say.

That phrase, "I am not," kept going through my head, because in one way I wasn't anymore, but in another, I kept on being.

"William!" Stacey slung a bag of groceries onto the floor, then snapped off the TV. "Have you ever considered what you're going to do with yourself? Your *life*? You've been here five weeks. Do you think we are going to get anywhere with you just sitting in front of the television? Look, the cleaning and cooking is nice and all, but you need to get a job. I can't support you forever. Got it?"

Her tone startled me into remembering one of the few times Mira had gotten pissed off at me.

Being with Mira had gotten me a lot of attention. Girls smiled at me and seemed to whisper when I passed. The boys were more outspoken. "Hey, dude," this guy we called Shooter said. "I hear you've gotten into the *forbidden territory*." The gesture he made wasn't pretty.

My stomach turned. I wanted to punch him, but I'd never started a fight in my life, although I'd finished a few. I decided to play dumb. "What do you mean?"

"You know, the ice queen. The polar princess. I heard you were doing her."

My mind swung to Ms. Ross. Maybe her "women are not objects" lecture wasn't as out there as I'd thought.

"Man, if I were doing anyone, I'd know it," I finally replied.

Then there was the response from my friends about all the time Mira and I spent together. Like when Cory called me in the spring, all excited because he'd scored a couple of six-packs from his uncle. "Hey, invisible man, we're heading to Narragansett Beach to hang. Just the guys," he added.

Cory, Bud, Jacks, and I had been friends since fourth grade, when our respective elementary schools had poured into one middle school. We'd played sports together, done Boy Scouts, gotten into plenty of trouble of a minor sort. At some point, Bud and Jacks split off a bit. They were wilder, drank harder, smoked pot. Cory and I became more of a unit.

I felt uneasy because Mira and I usually got together after school, but I said, "Cool."

After I hung up, I called Mira. "Hey, how are you?"

"Good, except I'm trying to make it through my *East of Eden* paper, and I'm stuck on the thesis. You've read it, right?"

Yeah, I'd read it; it was one of my favorites. It was about two brothers, Adam and Charles, and a completely evil woman: Cathy, a murderess and prostitute.

"I mean, that Bible thing has been done so many times.

Sibling rivalry. Cain and Abel. Adam and Eve. I'm trying to find a different slant. God, I hope your mom didn't name you after *that* Adam. He was so *dense*."

"Well, when's it due?"

"Tomorrow. But I've made a lot of progress. I can spend an hour on it, and then we can go downtown or something. This is like the first warm weekend in months. I'll make a picnic. The maid just went shopping, and my fridge is full of all kinds of cool stuff, even imported truffles. The mushroomy kind, not the chocolate."

"Uh . . . did we have plans?"

There was a long silence. "What?"

"Cory and Jacks asked me to go surfing tonight, so I thought I might . . ."

"You're standing me up?"

"I just . . ."

"You just *what*?"

"I just thought I'd hang out with the guys tonight. I didn't think we had plans."

Her voice came out like burning ice, if such a thing were possible: "No we didn't have 'plans.' What we had was an expectation. We've gotten together every single day for almost a month. I've waited for you to get off work, I've stayed up way later than I should have, and my schoolwork is suffering. Like, why isn't my paper done? Because I helped you shelve books last night until midnight. Remember?"

"Yeah."

"I could've made other plans if I'd known you were going to bag on me. There are other people who want to spend time with me, you know."

I tried to think about the logic of the situation, to put myself in her place. "Look, it's just one night."

"Maybe not, Adam. Maybe it's not just one night."

"What do you mean?" My stomach twisted.

"I'll find someone else to take me on a picnic tonight."

After she hung up, I stared at the phone. It was like I was waiting for it to speak to me and tell me what to do. Instead it rang, louder than it ever had, it seemed. I jumped.

"My man. All set?" Cory's voice.

"I can't go."

"What?"

"Mira's pissed. We had plans for tonight."

"Jesus, Adam. Big fucking deal. You're with Mira twenty-four seven. Me and Jacks feel like you fell off the planet or were captured by space aliens like on that episode of *Arthur*. Remember *Arthur*? We used to watch it together all the time in middle school."

"I remember."

"And we didn't tell anyone else because it was a little kid show. Remember that?"

"What is this, a guilt trip?"

"Come on, Adam. Loosen up. We don't even have a way to get there. And your dad's cool about you using the car."

"Not after you puked in it."

"I'm better at holding my liquor now. I swear."

"Another time."

"You're a pussy, you know that? You're pussy-whipped and a pussy."

I sighed, feeling as pinned down as I had in any wrestling match. "How 'bout I come over and kick your ass, and then we can decide who's a pussy." I said it like I meant it. "I will if you want me to."

There was a long silence. Then, "Meow. Okay? Happy? Want me to purr?"

I laughed. "Sorry, dude. I really am. We'll get together soon."

"Yeah, right."

"I promise."

"Yeah. Yeah. Truth be told, I'd choose to spend the evening with a babe like that over us morons too."

When I called Mira back, she was crying. "I'm sorry," she said. "You can go with your friends. I was being a bitch. It's just, I'm premenstrual, and I, like, get . . . carried off."

I pictured her floating away on a river of blood.

"It's okay. I canceled with them."

"It's not okay. I can get wicked mean when I'm on my period. I wouldn't go out with anyone else. Don't break up with me, okay?"

"Never," I said, and meant it.

I asked my mom about the period business.

"Yeah, menstruation stinks. Think about it: If a man bled that much from a part of *his* body, he'd be rushing to the emergency room."

Stacey didn't soften toward me any that night or apologize, though. She just glared at me over the pasta I made, then told me to sleep on the floor.

CHAPTER 9

elongate:
to lengthen, to prolong.

The next day, I started working at the diner. I was both the busboy and the dishwasher, running between the two stations. The owner of the diner was typecast for the part, a three-hundred-pound beast they called Sid the Terrible. He snarled at the waitresses and ate off the customers' plates before he sent them out. The only person he was cool with was his son, Rad. Rad tended the cash register. Only family got into that drawer, Sid informed me.

Since I didn't have an identity, I worked just for tips. The first day, after an eight-hour shift, I made sixteen dollars.

Aside from the low pay, which Stacey pocketed for my share of our expenses, the problem was Rad. Stacey told Rad that I could hear but not talk—a childhood speech problem, she fabricated. But Rad couldn't get it through his head that I wasn't deaf. He made a stash of wadded-up paper and threw it at me to get my attention, which he seemed to need about a hundred times a day. When he ran out of paper, he switched to objects. He'd throw spoons, paper clips, anything he could get his hands on. "We're out of coffee mugs, moron," he'd yell once he got my attention. "Let's speed things up."

The waitresses, Sid, everyone seemed to think it was funny to see Rad turn me into human target practice, but it was getting under my skin. I don't like bullies, never have, and I've never put up with one. A feeling entered the numbness of my body. It was the sensation I would have at the beginning of a wrestling match. My mom jokingly called it testosterone mind, a play on "Buddha mind," the feeling of peace after meditation or yoga. She said it the few times she caught Dad and me watching hockey or football. She said it when I was eight and she found out that Dad was teaching me to box. She said it when I wanted to join the wrestling team.

"Why do you want to fight with people?"

"I'm lousy at baseball," I said.

"What about basketball," she suggested, "if you have to do a sport? You're tall enough."

"Yeah. I'm just not into it."

She sighed. "Wrestling . . ."

"It's better than football."

"It's kind of sexual, you know that," she smirked. "Two guys grabbing each other and rolling around."

"Homosexual." I went with it.

"If you turn gay from all these manly sports, I'll accept you and I'll still love you."

"Yeah, right." I laughed, although I knew it was quite true; she'd love me if I turned into a poodle. My mom was one of those people who thought the word "liberal" was a high compliment.

"Testosterone mind." She sighed and signed the consent form.

So I wasn't cool about Rad, but what could I do? The only way to stop a bully is to show him you can't be bullied. Usually words do the trick. But I didn't have them.

One day I looked at the greasy calendar in the kitchen. Sid the Terrible had marked off each day as if he actually expected something would happen. It was June 20. I blinked at the date. School was over. I'd missed the last seven weeks of my junior year. *Go home.* The words popped into my head. It was the first time I'd thought about it, but it wouldn't be the last.

The spatula made a *thwack* as it hit the back of my neck. "Get with it, powder puff," Rad shouted. "You gotta find the lentil in the ashes if you wanna go to the ball."

I looked at him.

"Because of Stacey, you get to come to my party," he explained.

CHAPTER 10

solenoid:
a coil of wire that becomes magnetic when an
electrical current is passed through it.

Rad's trailer brought to mind every car-chase movie I'd ever seen, and every bar I'd passed that stank of beer. It was a half trailer, really, the kind you'd hitch to the back of a truck. It rested in the parking lot of the diner, so close to the highway that it shook whenever a truck roared by.

The place was full of kids. I wondered where they'd come from. In all the weeks I'd been there I hadn't ventured farther than the motel, just down the road. The world had shrunk to asphalt. I guessed there must be a town nearby with schools, a library, a hardware store.

Aside from a beat-up gold tweed couch and a side table made out of bricks and plywood, there wasn't any furniture—just a portable CD player and a keg.

Some girls were dancing in the middle of the room. They looked pretty wasted. A couple was making out on the couch as if they were the only ones there.

Stacey pulled me forward. "Try to socialize," she scolded. "Okay? Don't just stare at everyone like you're . . . superior. You're not superior. You just don't talk. There's nothing superior about that."

She crossed to the keg, poured a couple of beers, handed me one, and walked away. Over the last week or two, she'd grown more and more fed up with me. It must have been pretty frustrating having an anonymous boyfriend who never talked.

In a second, she reappeared and joined the dancing girls. I stood by myself and watched her dance for a while, then went toward the back of the trailer. There was one tiny bedroom with a sleeping bag in it and a radio. I went in and closed the door, then turned the radio on and put it to my ear.

I listened to the local news stories: a cow escaping its paddock and walking down the main street of town, a man beating his wife and being hauled to jail, a farm stand closing, a grocery store opening.

Life went on, it seemed, whether it had stopped for me or not.

I listened for an hour, until hunger drove me back to the party. By then the trailer was completely packed.

"Hey." A guy appeared. He was as tall as me, but the skinniest guy I've ever seen, with so many piercings, I couldn't count them. In one hand he had a cigarette; in the other, a joint. He alternated puffing on them. "You're the guy who doesn't talk, right? A vow of silence, Stacey said."

Stacey was fond of making up stories to explain my muteness. This was a new one.

I nodded. At least it was better than a childhood speech impediment. And I was glad to have someone to "talk" with.

"I tried that," the guy said. "You know?"

I nodded, though I didn't.

"I even gave up grass and booze so I wouldn't be . . . *compelled* to express myself. I was listening to Pink Floyd. Shit from our grandparents' day, but good shit. *The Dark Side of the Moon*. And it came to me—revelation—that all the crap in the world is from people blathering on and on. Blah blah blah. And saying the wrong thing. So I took this vow of silence, man, knowing it would bring me inner peace and solve my problems with authority. Like, if I didn't tell the teacher to fuck off, I'd probably graduate and all."

He offered me the joint. I shook my head, held up my beer.

"I mean, think about it. No one speaks, so there are no arguments, no battles, no wars. Love can be expressed through *touch*. Right? Words don't serve anything."

I nodded. He had a point.

"I tell my friends I'm leaving town, which I am in a way, and I start. I'm quiet in my room for, like, three hours, and it's totally blissful. But then the phone rings, which is fine. No problem, because I'm not answering it. But my mom is like, get this, in the shower. And she's got a freakin' *obsession* with the phone and the mail. It's like she thinks something decent is finally going to happen in her miserable life through one of these venues. The phone rings and she screams, 'Bobby! Answer the phone!' I don't. 'Bobby!' I stay silent. Finally, she shrieks, 'Answer the goddamned phone or I'm taking your car away for six months!' So I had to answer it. I'm like . . . 'Hello.' And it's a goddamned telemarketer. And I've blown it because I'm like . . . 'Hello.' So that was it."

I nodded to show sympathy.

"I'm gonna try it again, though. Definitely. On my vacation week."

I gave him the thumbs-up sign.

"Ever try to thread a needle when you're stoned?" He took a hit off his joint. "It's a totally different experience. To get that thread through that little hole. The *eye* of the needle. Like it can see something. You know? That's what it's called. The *eye.*"

I nodded.

"I'm gonna go find a needle and thread. Stay put. I want to see you try this."

He disappeared.

On a nice summer night like this, Mira and I might have gone into Newport and eaten at an outdoor café, then caught a late flick at the Jane Pickens, the old theater that plays independent flicks. Or we might have gone to a clambake on the beach and swum in the ocean. What I'd have liked to do now was find the town and go for a nice meal with Stacey, a movie, something normal.

I went into the kitchen. Stacey was there with Rad, his arm around her waist. When she saw me, she jumped away from him. "We were just . . ." she started.

". . . about to make it," Rad finished.

She slugged him.

"We used to be together," she explained.

I knew I was supposed to be mad or jealous, but I couldn't summon it. All I felt was hunger. The last time I'd eaten was breakfast.

"And we'll be together again," Rad threatened.

I felt myself shrug—a mistake.

"You could care less," Stacey snapped at me. She stormed out.

I started to go after her, but this kid came in and patted me on the shoulder like he knew me. "Dude." He held up a bottle of tequila. "I found it."

"Gimme that." Rad grabbed it from him and poured a shot. I looked out the window. It was almost dark. The highway was right there like a black stream. It lit up every time a car or truck came along. The motel was on the same road, about three miles away. I figured I could just walk it.

As I turned to leave, an empty beer can hit me in the

back of the head. When Rad threw something at me, it was always when my back was turned. I jerked around. "Move on from Stacey, powder puff," he said.

I remembered how much it used to bug Mira when boys used female words to disparage other boys.

"What's so bad about having feminine traits? At least women don't start wars."

"How about Helen of Troy?" I argued.

"It was fought over her, but she didn't start it."

"What do *girls* do with their anger?" I asked.

"They punish each other psychologically." She sighed. "They snub each other, gossip, start rumors, lie. To tell you the truth, I'd prefer a punch in the eye any time."

"You hear me, deafo?" Rad moved toward me. *Tequila bravery*, I thought. The other guy chuckled under his breath like Beavis or Butt-head.

I shrugged and held up my hands, a gesture of acquiescence. It didn't work. Rad grabbed the front of my shirt.

I sighed. I sighed like Mom did every time Margarite called and told her of her latest failure with a man. I sighed the way she did when George Bush told Americans Saddam was hiding weapons of mass destruction, and they believed him. I sighed because I knew that I couldn't snub him, or gossip, or do anything as easy as that. I was going to have to fight.

Words popped into my head. Thoughts coalesced more than they had been. I thought, *war, peace, peace vigil*. I thought, *Go home, Adam. William is not really your name.*

"Come on, motherfucker." Rad hissed out the ugliest phrase in the English language. His breath stank of tequila. "What are you scared of?"

I wasn't scared. I was considering my options. The way I figured it, I had two: box or wrestle. It always came down to that. Boxing *was* violence, no doubt about it. Damage occurred: a split lip, a bloody nose, a blackened eye. Wrestling was more of a dance. Boxing got adrenalin pumping and it didn't stop until someone was beaten. A wrestling hold could decrease the excitement and relax things.

Rad shoved me toward the kitchen counter. But I kept my balance and shot my leg forward, caught his arm, and moved into a head and arm lock. Since he was drunk, he didn't stand his ground at all, but tumbled sideways. I yanked him forward, then took him down and pinned him in a full leg nelson, my leg caught under his shoulder and over his neck. I pressed hard so that his face was smashed into the floor—an illegal move. I glanced up at the other guy, Rad's buddy, wondering when he was gonna jump in or tackle me. If he did, Rad could get hurt. But the guy just poured another shot and watched us. It was like we were reality TV or something.

"You son of a bitch," Rad snarled. "You're fired. You know that, asshole!"

I was amused to be fired, since they paid me nothing but tips anyway.

Rad kept struggling, but his energy was going. And it felt good to have him pinned, to be doing something that took action.

Bobby came in, holding up a needle and thread, but when he saw the fight, he backed out of the room.

"Let go of me, you jerk," Rad whined. "You're gonna break my neck. You'll go to jail for assault."

Jail, I thought. *Who cares?* If I were in jail, at least I'd know where the hell I was, and what my future held. The thought startled me. Because if I was raised to do anything, it was to care.

"Giiive! I give!" Rad finally whined.

I loosened the hold a bit. His body was relaxing. Slowly, I let go of him, but I kept watching. I knew he might come up swinging.

He crawled toward his friend, then climbed to his feet, rubbing the back of his neck. "What the hell are you staring at?" he said to the guy.

The guy offered Rad a shot.

"Dumbass," Rad snarled at him, changing the direction

of his hostility. "I told you not to let me fight when I'm drunk. I'm not at my best!"

Through the window, I saw that a truck had pulled off on the side of the road. It was a huge one with pictures of fruit on the side.

"You can get the fuck out of my house," Rad said from his safe distance.

I nodded in agreement, backed out of the kitchen, and made my way out the door.

The truck's hood was up. The driver was peering at the engine. I crossed the road.

The guy looked like he'd lived hard. His face was deeply lined. Gray whiskers dotted his skin. "Something was knocking," he explained.

I stood there with him, waiting. "What the hell." He closed the hood.

I followed him to the cab.

"What is it?" he asked.

I shrugged.

"Need a ride?"

I nodded.

"I'm heading to Colorado."

I climbed into the passenger seat.

Sure, I was going to Colorado.

CHAPTER 11

radiant:
1. giving out rays of light. 2. looking very bright and happy.

The cab smelled like incense and something sweet; I couldn't figure out what.

"Cherries." The driver read my mind. "Smells nice at first, but boy do you get sick of it."

I smiled. The thought of a truckful of cherries made my mouth water.

The inside of the truck was like a shrine. There were candles stuck on the dashboard with melted wax, crosses hanging from the rearview mirror, and about fifty photographs, all of the same blond woman, glued to the doors and ceiling.

"So what was that? A party?"

I nodded.

"It was so crowded in that trailer that there were people sticking out of the window. I wouldn't be surprised if the thing toppled over. Reminds me of the old days when kids used to stuff themselves into phone booths. You're too young to remember that."

I peered up at the cheesy photo above my head. The blond woman was perched on a bear rug, topless.

"She's not here anymore," he said.

I felt like I'd been caught going through his drawers. I looked away.

"She's been gone twenty-seven years. Leukemia. But it's like last week. That's how clearly I remember her. Oh, how she shined. But hey. Who knows? Maybe she would've driven me crazy by now. She was a drinker and a smoker. Women look like shit when they smoke. Maybe she'd just be some boozy old dame with a wrinkled face, instead of young and beautiful forever. Maybe she'd be a cow." He wiped his eyes. "Don't you talk?"

I shook my head.

"You'll be better company, then. Right?" He laughed.

I smiled.

"That's some set of teeth you got."

My teeth stick out like my dad's. My parents once took me to an orthodontist to get a consultation about braces. The orthodontist droned on about surgery, headgear, and four years of tin mouth. My parents dutifully agreed. Then the guy gave the price: eight thousand dollars. Dad gulped. Mom got pale.

"Uh, do you have a credit plan?" Dad asked.

"Oh, yes," the orthodontist offered. "You can pay it over the first year at only one percent interest."

"Okay," my mom answered in a cheerful voice. "We'll do that. When do we get started?"

On the drive home, both my parents were silent, and so was I. Our car was a Pinto from the 1970s, the sides rusted out, half the fender missing. Aside from driving to the Cape and camping, we hadn't had a vacation for years. My parents were vegetarians; in spring and summer, they grew their own food. Without them really talking about it, I knew they were strapped; you don't get rich running a bookstore.

"Why do I have to have braces?" I leaned forward on the seat.

"To look handsomer than you already are, if that's possible," Mom said.

"Didn't the dentist say something about his bite?" Dad offered.

"Yes. And there's your bite."

"I can bite just fine," I said.

Mom laughed. "It will *improve* your bite."

"Dad's teeth are like mine, and he's fine. He can . . . bite."

"I can chew and swallow, too." He patted his stomach.

"I don't want the braces," I said. I knew not to mention the money.

There was a long silence.

"You're having them," Mom argued.

"He doesn't want them," Dad said.

"Yes, but he'll regret it later. Won't you regret it, Adam, when you're grown up and . . ."

"No," I said. "Braces are bullshit, another consumerist conspiracy to bilk parents."

Mom roared with laughter at that. "Boy, you're a real chip off the old block."

"Teeth and all," Dad added with relief.

"Fine," Mom agreed. "No braces."

The driver was talking, I realized. I tried to look like I'd been listening.

"Put mine in a glass at night, is what I do," he said. "Then I don't have to bother with 'em. But I can't eat corn on the cob anymore, that's for sure. Or beef jerky."

He lit a cigarette. I guess he thought they were okay for guys. My lungs are pretty sensitive; I was glad I'd cracked my window already.

"So where you headed?" he asked. "Trying to get home?"

I nodded.

"I guess we're all trying to get home—although I don't have a home, per se. I'm what you call a loner. Watch out for anything in a pack: coyotes, chain restaurants, church groups, clubs, lobbies, committees. 'Have no idols before ye,' it is said, but mine is the ocotillo, all alone in the desert and prickly."

The blond girl on the door stared at me from what

looked like a high-school photograph. Her face was sweet and sad, as if she knew the word "gone" was the closest relative to "time."

"You might as well sleep a bit," the driver suggested, turning the radio to a country station. "We'll be driving a good part of the night—'bout as long as that party will last."

The party. Yeah. Rad would have to find someone else to bully. And he would. The world was full of Rads. You only had to read a history book to figure that out. And at the root of every Rad was fear. "Out of the gamut of human emotions," Dad once said, "most of them suck."

I thought about Stacey, and what a shit I was to take off like that without explanation or good-bye.

As if in response to my feelings, a sign appeared on the highway: THANK YOU FOR VISITING IDAHO.

A knife went through me. I was leaving Idaho, abandoning my parents. They were still there, I imagined, lying together in the car, waiting for me to do what I was supposed to do: get them to a hospital, take them home, bury them.

I clenched my eyes shut against an intense wave of nausea, grateful that I hadn't eaten anything in about eight hours.

CHAPTER 12

arbitrary:
based on random choice or impulse.

I woke up to the smell of diesel fuel and to lights flashing into my eyes—a neon sign that said HOME COOKING.

"I'll drop you here," the driver informed me. "It'll be easier for you to get another ride."

I blinked in the darkness. We were in Colorado already? I didn't know if I'd slept thirty minutes or thirty hours.

"You gonna be okay?" he asked.

Oh, yeah. I was gonna be great.

I jumped down from the rig.

"Good luck, Pal," he said.

I gave a fakely cheerful wave. I was on my own again, not a good feeling.

The truck stop was as busy as if it were daylight: the pumps lit up, the diner filled with truckers. I could smell the food wafting through the air: meat loaf, mashed potatoes and gravy, cherry pie.

I wished I had thought things through better. Like, I could have gone back to the motel and packed some food, or at least had a meal before I set off. I could've gotten some money from Stacey, and said good-bye.

I stared into the windows of the diner, at all the forks and spoons being lifted so easily to mouths; then I searched my pockets as if dollars would magically appear. Finally, I walked to the exit and stuck my thumb out. The ground was wet, like the place had been hosed down. When trucks passed, water sprayed up at me.

To occupy myself, I tried to remember every great meal I'd ever had: my first bite of meat ever, with Bud's family at the Portuguese American Club steak fry; the summer clambakes at Third Beach; Mira's cilantro shrimp and savory bread pudding. I remembered how food at our house improved after I started going out with her.

The first time Mira came to dinner at our house, Mom made her "famous" lentil casserole and an iceberg salad with alfalfa sprouts and mayonnaise dressing. Mom's cooking was something Dad and I felt was best not talked about. Once and once only, Dad suggested that Mom check out the cookbook section of our shop. "Why?" she asked. "Food is so . . . boring."

He slid me a glance. I looked the other way.

"Don't you guys like my cooking?" She sounded hurt.

"No. No, it's great," Dad assured her. "Better than mine, anyway."

64

"Adam?"

"Well, you know me. I like meat and all, but otherwise, it's fine."

"You're sure?"

"Yeah."

"Sure," Dad echoed.

Mom stared us down until we both went back to our tasks. "Food," she mumbled. "What's to read about?"

Mira wasn't quite so tactful. She took a couple of swallows of lentils and her eyes got wide. "Have you got any . . . rice vinegar? Or . . . Tabasco sauce, maybe?" she asked hopefully.

We didn't.

The second time she came, she barged right into the kitchen. "What's cooking?"

"Tofu scramble, cabbage, and rye toast. Taste." Mom offered Mira a spoonful of tofu. It looked like gray scrambled eggs.

Mira tasted. She had to work hard not to make a face. "Tell you what, Mrs. Walton," she suggested. "You bring out all the spices you have, an onion, and some garlic, and let me just . . . work on this a bit."

"Really?" Mom peered over at me. "Well, that should be fun."

"I'm going to be a chef," Mira confided. "Did Adam tell you?"

I hadn't, since Mira had never told *me*.

Mom pulled out all the spices she had, which consisted of salt, pepper, and something called Spike.

A couple of days later, Mira showed up with a bag of stuff from her house. After that, she was the chef at our house on the nights she was there. Mom's tofu scramble became sesame ginger tofu. Mom's baked gluten became spicy basil gluten with roasted garlic. I didn't know who was more grateful, Dad or me.

The darkness thinned. To the east, a strip of pale light expanded. In the light, I noticed a group of people congregating in the corner of the parking lot. It was as if they were waiting for a bus, only there didn't seem to be a stop.

As I walked over to them, I realized that they were Hispanic, all of them. One of the men turned to look at me. He wore a straw hat and a T-shirt that said FRANK. I wondered if it was his name or a statement about his personality. "Gringo." Frank smiled. "*¿Qué pasa?*"

In answer, my stomach growled loudly.

He chuckled, dug into his pocket, and pulled out a Snickers. There was half of it left. He shrugged, an apology, and handed it to me. I smiled in thanks and scarfed it down.

We stood there about an hour. I knew I should head off and try to hitch a ride, but being with the group made me feel safe. Unlike the trucker, I wanted to be part of a pack.

Finally, a pickup screeched to a halt in front of us. The man in the passenger seat jumped out. He pointed at different people: "You, you, you, you." He started to go, but then the driver said something to him. He turned back and pointed to Frank and then to me. "You two."

Frank climbed onto the back of the truck, then he motioned for me to follow. *"Vamos."*

CHAPTER 13

ersatz:
serving as a substitute.

We worked the day in the fields. The work was grueling, especially for me, who wasn't used to bending all day in the hot sun, who didn't have a hat, whose hands were white and soft—shop hands—and who hadn't had food in my body since yesterday, except for half a Snickers.

I went back to my dreams of Mira's cooking. There were her crepes, her white-chocolate-dipped strawberries, that amazing blueberry pie she made for Fourth of July.

That was when Mira finally let me see her arms— the day she told me her parents hated her, and I didn't believe her.

The picnic was at Third Beach in Newport. It was about ninety degrees, and Mira was wearing a long-sleeved pink shirt over a yellow bikini. "Aren't you hot?" I asked.

"Boiling."

"Let's swim."

"Okay." She stood up and headed for the water.

"Aren't you going to take off your shirt?"

"Nah," she joked. "There's not much there to see."

"Is that what you . . ."

"What?"

"You always wear long sleeves."

"So."

I shook my head. "Never mind."

"I keep my arms hidden, you know, like Muslim women do their heads."

I laughed, but she looked serious.

"Why?" I finally asked.

She crossed her arms in front of her and pulled up the shirt. The skin around the yellow bikini top was paper white. Her arms were still covered, though. "Adam . . ."

"Yes?"

"How long have we been going out?"

"Four months or so. Why?"

"I remember you in seventh grade," she said. "That was when I first saw you. When you would wrestle, your mom and dad came and watched you. Your mom covered her eyes when things got tough. Between matches, she'd wave like mad at you. Then you'd wave back, all dorky and unselfconscious."

"Gee, thanks."

"I thought . . . if I could climb inside his clothes, just flatten myself against him like a paper doll, then maybe I would feel that secure, that comfortable."

"You can put yourself inside my clothes. That's cool with me," I joked.

She pulled off her shirt. Her arms from the wrist to the forearms were covered in scars: gashes, as if she'd made hundreds of suicide attempts with a small razor blade.

"What happened? Did you . . ."

"Try to kill myself? Nah. Not literally. I just . . . used to, you know, make cuts . . ."

"You cut yourself?"

"Yep."

"But why?"

"The usual reason. To feel something. To slash through the numbness. To get at my mom, who has to have everything be so perfect, to have me be perfect."

"How long did this go on?"

"About two years. Then I stopped."

"What made you stop?"

She shrugged. "I don't know. Maybe it was because she gave up on me."

"Your mom?"

"Yeah. She couldn't believe that she raised a daughter who didn't want to have a coming-out party, or to spend weekends at the country club. She felt cheated that we didn't have mother-daughter spa weekends or shopping sprees. When she told me the name of a designer I should wear, I thought she was talking about a disease. I could tell you stories about being dragged to cotillions, parties, pageants, recitals, you name it, and doing things to deliberately embarrass her. But one day, when I was about fifteen, she decided I was an alien and stopped trying. It's such a cliché."

"An alien?" I laughed.

"Yeah. Like, from another planet."

"No way."

"Way. That's what she calls me. Alien." She held her arms toward me like a surrender. "Gross, huh?"

"No." I kissed her wrists and forearms. "It's not gross."

"Variation on a theme of tattoos," she said. Then she threw the shirt back on, ran to the ocean, and dove in.

After what felt like twelve hours, the workers got to break for lunch. We were fed chili, corn bread, and iced tea. I don't think anything has ever tasted better.

I sat off on my own until Frank motioned me over. He grabbed my hand and held it up to show an older man. The blisters had turned into raw, oozing holes. The old man shook his head disapprovingly. He pulled a small tube out of his pocket and squeezed salve onto the blisters. It stung like hell, but after a couple of minutes, the area went numb.

After we ate, we were allowed to rest a few minutes in the shade. One of the men took out a harmonica and started to play a tune. Frank mimed the action of playing a guitar. I could tell he really knew how to play. Soon, they were all singing. The music was beautiful and sad. I don't know Spanish, but I was sure the songs were about love, and that the love never turned out the way it was supposed to.

A feeling rose in me, of comfort. I was part of them, like a family. I would stay with them forever.

But that feeling was immediately replaced by fear. Or maybe it was a premonition: that what was so easily gained could be lost in an instant. That anything could be lost in an instant.

CHAPTER 14

contretemps:
an unfortunate happening.

The second half of the day was harder. Although the wounds were now numb, my hands felt stiff and immobile. I'd eaten way too much, too fast. In the heat, my full stomach made me feel like I was moving in molasses. Worse was the anxiety I felt. What would I do at the end of the day when the Mexicans went home? Would Frank invite me to join him? Would I sleep in the fields? Would I make enough to rent a motel room?

The foreman, the guy who'd invited us onto the truck, walked through the fields to check on the work. *"Bueno. Bueno,"* he said. Until he got to me. "You're slow," he told me. "Much slower than the rest. How'd you get in with the Mexicans, anyway?"

In answer, I tried to speed up. I didn't even bother looking up at him. I put my thoughts back on Mira.

I'd gone out with Mira for almost a year before I met her parents. She preferred hanging out with my family; I'd soon learn why.

Her house was unbelievable, a giant wedding cake perched on the edge of a cliff, complete with a tree-lined drive, stables, tennis courts, and an Olympic-size pool. The inside was cavernous, with a hall that seemed as big as my whole house, marble floors, and a long, winding staircase.

We met her dad first. He peered up at us from behind glasses, a pipe, and a giant desk in the library. He looked like he didn't recognize either of us.

"Daddy, this is Adam," Mira offered. "I've told you about him."

"Ah, the swimmer?" Her dad searched his memory.

Mira frowned and folded her arms. "There's never been a swimmer."

"No? What's your last name, young man?"

"Walton, sir," I said. I had a feeling I should say "sir."

"Of course. From the Connecticut Waltons?" he asked.

"No, from the TV Waltons," Mira sniped. "You know. Mountain people? John Boy and hound dogs?"

"Nice to meet you, sir." I offered my hand.

"Good. Good." He shook my hand. "Mountain people. Bottled water. Healthy stuff. Perrier, is it? No, that's from France. Poland Spring?"

I had no idea what he was talking about.

"We're going to study now." Mira pulled me away.

"Got to keep up those grades," he called after us.

"He needs to think you're from an important family," she explained. "He does that about everything. It has to be grandiose. Alcohol-related dementia."

"I do feel like I'm on a TV show," I joked, "but it's definitely not *The Waltons*."

"*The Apprentice*," she joked. "It gets worse."

Getting worse meant meeting her mom, I knew.

We found her in a walk-in closet as big as my bedroom. She was trying on various pairs of lavender shoes. She looked exactly like Joan Rivers, give or take a few face lifts, a stick figure in talk-show attire: a lavender tweed suit, pearls, and a diamond ring the size of my fist.

"So . . ." she began. The expression on her face was not pleasant. "You're the alien's boyfriend?"

I felt my jaw drop open.

"See." Mira gloated.

Her mom was nonplussed. "You look a lot more normal than I thought you would, all things considered. I figured you'd be pierced or tattooed or have spiked green hair. Or . . . what is that word? 'Goth'?"

"Thank you," I said.

"What are you thanking me for?"

"For, uh, having me over."

"It's the alien who's having you over."

I couldn't believe it. It was just like she said. Her mom thought she was an alien. Her dad wasn't the least bit interested in either of us. The taste of envy I'd felt when I saw the house melted in my mouth.

She turned to Mira. "Which of these shoes do you think matches this suit?"

"They're all exactly the same color." Mira's voice was tense.

"There are variations on the *shades*, actually, but you have to have a subtle eye to catch it."

"I'd wear those barf-green ones." Mira pointed to a hanging bag full of lime-green shoes. "Or is it booger green? Come on, Adam."

Mira led me away. "Well, what would you expect from an alien," her mom mumbled, then she yelled after us, "Do not close the door to your room!"

We headed up the stairs. My back felt prickly. I half expected her mom to throw spiked heels after us.

"Did I tell you?" Mira's voice was shaky.

"Wow." It was all I could say. As fancy as the place was, I could see why she didn't want to be home.

The man next to me stopped working. I looked up and saw that several others had stopped too. They were staring off in the distance to where a brown truck had driven up. Two men in uniform got out of it and started wandering slowly toward the foreman.

Frank called out to the others in a low voice, and they returned to their work, but a couple of men started running. The uniformed men took chase. "Shit," Frank cursed. It was the first word I'd heard him say in English.

The foreman approached us then. He shouted instructions in Spanish and gestured to everyone to line up. "Not you," he said, when I joined them.

The cops returned with one man. The other had gotten away. The first cop was white. He reminded me of a tractor. He had a fullback's build, and his body moved in one piece when he turned. He had the mean look that some TV cops have. The other cop was older and Hispanic. He just looked sad and tired. "*Documentos*," he demanded.

Two of the workers produced worn cards from their pockets and were sent back to the fields. None of my group had papers, though. Not one of them.

Frank, the older man who'd dressed my hands, and six others were led to the brown truck. I wanted to go with them wherever they were going, back to Mexico, to jail, even. I just didn't want to be left on my own again.

"Go back to work, kid," the older cop warned, as I followed them. "This doesn't concern you."

I wanted to say something, anything, to object, but of course, I couldn't. I was silent and useless.

"Get lost, hippie." The mean cop gave me a shove. "Go commune with your plants."

Hippie? Then I realized that my hair was pretty long. It had been months since I'd had a haircut. At least I'd shaven at Stacey's.

Frank gave me a nod, as if to tell me it was okay. He'd be back. I'd listen to him sing again and share a candy bar.

I backed away enough to placate the cop, then watched my friends being led to the van and caged, the door slamming behind them.

CHAPTER 15

caterwaul:
to utter long wailing sounds.

I didn't go back to the fields. I couldn't see the point. Instead, I chased after the van and watched it shrink and disappear down the road.

I wondered if they'd be thrown in jail or just sent back to Mexico. They hadn't even collected their pay for the half day's work. Neither, for that matter, had I.

The sun was still high. I figured I had a few hours before I'd have to find a safe place to sleep. My shoes were already worn to the treads. If they were tires, they'd have popped and sent me skidding off the road.

I wasn't hitching. I was nothing. I wanted to be nothing. But only a few minutes after I started out, a truck pulled over, like magic, and waited on the side of the road in front of me. A low mournful sound that reflected my feelings came from it.

Sheep. The truck was full of them. I could see their fluffy backs through the slats. People say that sheep go, "Baaa," but it's much more plaintive than that. The beginning letter is an *M*, not a *B*. "Maaa," they moan, calling for their mothers.

"You need a ride?" the driver yelled from the window. There were two children and a woman squeezed in beside him. The woman gave me a dirty look.

I nodded.

"Where you headed?" he asked.

"He don't talk!" the girl sneered.

As impolite as she was, she was right.

"He's dumb," the boy said. "A dummy."

"This is the hottest June on record." The driver ignored his rude kids. "And it's going to be even hotter in Texas."

Texas, I thought. *South.* But it was also east. I nodded.

"You'll have to get in with the sheep. We don't have no more room in here. If you can handle that, you're on your way."

Riding with sheep wasn't as bad as I'd have thought. They smelled bad and made a racket, but they kept pretty much to themselves. Besides, the slats added a breeze and a place for me to pee when I had to go.

The sheep were not as polite. They just went where they stood. It made the ride a game of dodgeball. Still, I was better off than my Mexican friends. The van hadn't had any windows.

We drove for a long time. The mountainous richness of Colorado gave way to nondescript highway, then endless desert and cactus. *Texas*, I thought. The biggest state. Home of cowboys, steak, concealed weapons, and the president my mom hated more than anyone on earth. It was not a place that attracted me.

Once it got dark, we pulled off the highway, and I watched the family go into a diner. They didn't ask me to join them; they didn't even check on me. To them I guess I was just one more sheep.

When I woke up, it was light. That kept happening. Dark and light. The truck was stopped. I was curled up next to a sheep, my head in its fluff. My stomach was growling. My hands were stinging again. I felt like I was about eighty years old.

The driver knocked on the slats. "We're heading home," he shouted. "You should wait here for your next ride."

I gave the sheep a few good-bye pats. I hoped they wouldn't end up on somebody's table.

The truck rattled off. I waved at the family as they drove off, but I was pretty sure none of them looked back at me.

CHAPTER 16

puissance:
great power or strength.

After we met her mom that day, Mira's whole personality seemed to change. I followed her into her bedroom. She slammed the door, then kicked it, adding a hole to where there were numerous others. "This house is built like junk," she said. "See how easy it is to destroy."

I was speechless. I'd never seen Mira so angry.

"It's weird." She plopped down on her bed. "They always seem worse when I have a witness."

"They're not that bad," I lied. "Your dad was pretty friendly."

"Yeah. He's always friendly when he's drunk."

"He didn't seem drunk."

She punched a pillow. "They're going to leave me their money after they drink themselves to death. And there's one thing I promise."

"What?"

"I'm giving it away. Every penny of it. I will not take a cent for myself."

"You can give it to me," I joked.

"We'll still be together, so I guess I could."

I kissed her. "I'm glad to hear we'll still be together."

Mira's room was all white. Her bed was round, with mosquito netting draped all around it. She kissed me back, passionately, then started to unbutton my shirt. "Adam, let's . . ."

"What?"

"You know . . ."

"What about your parents?" My heart was pounding. There was part of me that couldn't believe my luck. I'd never pressed it about sex. I didn't want to do anything that would screw up the relationship. I figured it would happen at the right time.

"They don't care." She had that same look on her face as she'd had in the locker room that day, like she wanted to show everyone how stupid they were.

"I don't think we . . ."

"What?"

"I don't think we should be doing this," I said.

"Why not?"

"It's not the right time, Mira."

She sat up. "You don't want to make love with me?"

"It's not that. You just seem . . ."

"Go!" She threw the pillow at me. "Get out!"

I couldn't believe it. In all the months we'd been together, almost every encounter had been marked by warmth and good humor. This was like, *Who are you? And what have you done with my girlfriend?*

"Go on. Leave."

My heart sank. My voice came out shaky. "I can't go."

"Why the hell not?"

"I don't have a car. You drove. We're about ten miles from my house." I started crying.

I felt stupid as hell, crying in front of her like that. But I wasn't crying because I had no way to get home, or because I hadn't gotten sex, or even because I'd just lost my girlfriend. I was crying because I couldn't imagine what it would be like to grow up with parents who were indifferent, who seemed even to hate you.

I probably hadn't cried since I was about eight, when our dog, Ralph Nader, got run over by a car. I felt pretty stupid about it.

"Adam." Mira rushed to me, put her arms around me. "I'm sorry."

The two most important words in the English language, my mom always said: *I'm sorry.*

"I just wanted . . ." I tried to explain. "When we make love the first time, I want it to be because it's right—not to get at your parents."

"I know, Adam. I know. It is to get at my parents, like

cutting myself. You're so wise. I always want to be with you. I want to live together like your parents. We'll work together and have a restaurant-bookstore. We'll have a greenhouse and grow our own vegetables. We'll read all the time and leave our coffee cups all over the house."

"It's a deal," I said, relieved as hell. And I meant it.

I stood on the road for a couple of hours. It wasn't desert any more, just a flat expanse of low bushes, scraggly trees. The gritty road slicing through it seemed incongruous, like a bulldozer in a rainforest.

I had no idea where I was, or which direction I should be going. There wasn't a car in sight.

Would I ever see a traffic jam again, the tollbooth at the Newport Bridge, or I-95 leading into Providence with its standstill line of cars? Or was it my fate to stare down long empty roads?

I looked at my watch. It said 6:23. But it seemed too light to be that early in the morning.

"Wait," the driver had said. But I didn't want to wait. I needed to get home, even if I had to hoof it the whole way.

I heard a car coming. I turned to hitch, but the driver ignored my outstretched hand. I wondered if my filthy shirt and torn jeans had anything to do with it. Or my long hair.

It was already hot. If I stayed out here long enough, I imagined I could burn up like an insect on glass.

Through one sparse copse of trees, I noticed a dirt path.

I wondered if it led to anything, even something unfriendly: a bear in a cave, a farmer with a shotgun, a raging river.

I turned down it, promising myself that I would walk for just a few minutes and not take any turns. I was afraid of getting lost.

I remembered a couple of books about people lost in the wilderness. One was *Hatchet*. We read it in fifth grade. It was about a kid in a plane crash who has to survive in the Canadian wilderness. Another was a true story about a college kid trapped in the woods in Alaska, called *Into the Wild*. The kid in *Hatchet* survives, but that's fiction. The guy in Alaska died.

The brush was getting denser. I turned to go back. But then I noticed a shack off the path, like a shoe box upended in the grass.

CHAPTER 17

wattle:
1. a structure of interwoven sticks and twigs used as material for fences, walls, etc. 2. a red fleshy fold of skin hanging from the head or throat of certain birds, as the turkey.

The outside walls were no more than boards nailed together. The roof was corrugated steel. Outside, there was an old cooler that said COCA-COLA, the kind of thing that used to hold sodas back when they came in glass bottles. I rushed over and opened it. There was nothing in it but a hammer, a crowbar, and a community of spiders.

I slammed the lid down. Attached to the wall was a pay phone. I grabbed the receiver. There was actually a dial tone. I tried to remember my phone number. I'd always had a good head for numbers—I kept the accounts for our store, and I aced math, even though I don't enjoy it, certainly not compared to English. But now, standing in the sweltering heat of what I assumed was Texas, I couldn't remember my own phone number.

It didn't matter. I didn't have any money.

I looked at my watch again. 6:23. Why, if time was going to freeze, could it not have frozen weeks ago, before we left on the trip? Why couldn't our car have died, or one of us have gotten food poisoning? Anything not to have let us leave home.

If Mom had been here, she would have blamed her death on George Bush, or the "House of Bush," as she called the father and son who seemed so careless about sending other people's children to war. There wouldn't have been a peace vigil. There would not have needed to be one.

The door to the shed was secured with a rusted padlock. Still, like an idiot, I knocked, as if someone would come out and invite me to tea.

No one answered. I went back to the cooler, hoping that an ice-cold Coke had magically appeared.

The crowbar. It was as if someone had left a key. But what would I find in the shed, even if I got in? A four-course meal? A nice warm bed? Shade? At least there was that. Maybe water.

The crowbar could have easily pried off the rusted lock, but I didn't pry. I swung at the lock. I battered it. And when it dropped to the ground, I whacked at it there in the dust like a maniac.

We'd broken into places a couple of times in eighth grade, me and Cory and Jacks and Bud, at that age when we were aching for something, anything to happen: for our bodies to grow to match our sudden, fiendish sexuality, for the world to notice our shining talents.

Instead, we stumbled pale-legged and scrawny through gym class, tried to hide ourselves when we showered, looked ten while the girls looked twenty, had acne and creaking voices. It was not pretty.

To compensate, we committed little crimes. We made dummies out of old clothes and hung them from the Mt. Hope Bridge, then laughed ourselves hoarse when it was reported as vandalism in the local paper. We climbed into the window of an abandoned house, spending an hour hoisting ourselves up and prying off the frame, only to find, once we were inside, that the house was missing the entire back wall, and we could have just wandered in from behind.

Cory raided his dad's liquor cabinet, his mom's stash of candy, and his brother's cigarette cartons; then we snuck into the cemetery and drank, ate, and smoked until we were sick. Bud wanted to switch all the flowers on the graves, but Cory and I couldn't bring ourselves to do something that mean.

We thought our restlessness could only be cured with something monumental.

In high school, Bud and Jacks started doing drugs and moving with a different crowd, but Cory and I settled down. I wrestled and worked more hours at the bookstore. Cory joined the jazz band and started working at his dad's car lot.

Our bodies grew to match the girls'. Our voices stopped cracking and we needed to shave. We started having a social life. We played volleyball at the beach in the summer and snowboarded in the winter. Everything was cool, except one night, I remember, our sophomore year, when Cory got upset in the car.

Cory was a year older, and he had his license. He had scored his brother's car. We had gone to a party in Tiverton. Most of the night, Cory stood around next to the sliding glass door, but I got into a game of cards with some girls and had a pretty good time.

"That was cool," I commented on the drive home.

"Cool for you," Cory sniped.

"You should've played cards with us."

"No one asked me."

"I did."

"The chicks didn't."

He sounded so pissed, I didn't say anything.

"You make me sick. Babes always go for you."

"No they don't," I argued.

"You're just too big a moron to realize it. Like that chick Lauren at the party. She looks like a model, and she was all over you."

"She was just playing around, trying to see my cards. We were wrestling."

He rolled his eyes. "It was her way of having sex with you. Ever read Freud?"

"She practically broke my arm!"

"Look, you're tall and good-looking. That's all chicks care about. Look at me. I'm five-four, skinny, and ugly. I was born this way, and there ain't nothing I can do about it. Do you know how hard it is to be a short guy?"

I didn't.

"It's like being a fat girl," he said. "Nobody takes you seriously. But at least a fat girl can lose weight."

"I don't think girls are like that," I said. "They don't just care about the surface."

"Trust me. They do. A guy like me, they think, 'Cool, he can be my *pal.*' If one more girl tells me what a great *friend* I am, I'm gonna deck her. I might as well be gay."

"Come on."

"Well, there's one other thing chicks dig, and that I can do something about."

"What?"

"Money. I'm gonna take me to law school and be a corporate lawyer or some shit, get rich, and drive a BMW."

"I guess you better start going to your classes," I told him.

"Yeah. No shit."

Cory was like that. He had a quick temper, but as quickly as he got mad, he laughed it off.

I left the battered lock and went to the door. It creaked as I pushed it open. *Trespassing. Breaking and entering.* Why the hell not?

I blinked to adjust my eyes, but compared with the light outside, it was pitch-dark. I slid inside. My lungs clenched up like a fist from the dust.

I knew there probably wouldn't be electricity in an abandoned shack, but I reached for a light switch anyway. A couple of splinters shot into my hand, but then I felt the switch. I flipped it, and nearly had a heart attack to join the asthma attack.

There, in the light, were eyes, about a hundred of them: wide and startled, marble, beady, and accusing.

I stood there, frozen, waiting for the bodies that held them to rise up and swoop for me, an avalanche of flapping wings and pecking beaks.

It took me at least a minute to figure out that the birds perched along the rows of tree branches were frozen in time and space, were not among the living.

I raised my eyes to the peeling sign above them, red paint on black: TAXIDERMY.

CHAPTER 18

scrutiny:
a careful look or examination of something.

The room reminded me of a classroom: that same organization, the specimens, the models of animals opened up to
show their skeletons.

School was okay as a social event, but most of the classes
were tedious, something to get through. Still, I would have
given anything to have been there now, to hear Bergeson's
whiny voice going on about ecosystems and natural selec-
tion, to have given a pat to Bessie, the human skeleton, whose
bones clanked like chimes when the window was open.

There were two or three stuffed deer heads mounted on the
wall, plus a moose head, and there was a bear rug sprawled on
the floor, like the one in the trucker's photo. But mostly there
were birds. I recognized some of them: hawks, owls, sparrows,
blue jays, and a solitary woodpecker. Their stillness made me
long for the live, shuffling bodies of the sheep. Beneath the
birds, under a dusty glass counter, were displays of feathers,

shells, and fossils, and a collection of butterflies pinned to cardboard. *House of the dead,* I thought. It was so creepy. Even the owner, I imagined, was not among the living.

I was about to leave when I noticed a small kitchen set-up at the back: a refrigerator, a microwave, and a sink.

First, I hit the sink. The water came out brown. I let it run for a while, then drank from it until I couldn't swallow any more.

Next, I opened the fridge. There was nothing in it, just a few cryptically labeled bottles that looked like urine specimens. The freezer held a jackpot, though: a pizza. The expiration date was two years ago, but I didn't care. I hadn't eaten since the chili with the Mexicans the day before.

I ripped off the carton and plastic wrapper and opened the microwave, then got another shock. A rat, gray and sinister, bared its teeth at me, like an imitation of the bear. You'd think I would have known, but it took me a couple of minutes to figure out that it, too, was stuffed.

I shuddered. To me, birds are best in the sky, insects on the other sides of screens, and animals either pettable or roaming in their own habitat. Rats definitely belonged outside.

I found a piece of cloth on the counter, removed the rat, and threw it in the trash; then I wiped out the microwave. I plopped the pizza in, trying not to think about rat juice or rodent preservative, then pressed the button. Nothing happened. I checked the plug and tried again.

I wasted about half an hour on microwave resuscitation

before giving up. I grabbed the pizza and hurled it like a Frisbee across the room. It hit the wall and crashed to the floor.

Then I got a new idea. Outside, the sun was shining in full force. I grabbed the pizza, took it outside, and laid it on the cooler to thaw.

I went back inside, cleaned up, washed my hair, then put my shirt in the sink. I kept my pants on, as much as I wanted to wash them. If someone showed up, I didn't want to be naked. The birds watched me from their perch as if they didn't like what they saw.

On the other side of the glass case were drawers. I searched through them. Most had medical-looking instruments, tools of the trade. One drawer was full of glass eyeballs. Another contained feathers. The last drawer had paper clips, rubber bands, markers, and seven quarters. I knew I needed the quarters for something, but my brain kept short-circuiting. I wondered if I'd ever think straight again in my life. I put the quarters in my pocket along with a marker and a few rubber bands to tie back my hair.

There were three clocks on the wall, but they didn't help me any. Like my watch, the birds, the butterflies, and my life, they were frozen in time and space.

CHAPTER 19

**litany:
a form of prayer consisting of a series of
supplications to God.**

I've always been a bit secretive about how I do in school. It's a guy thing. As early as fourth grade I remember the girls gushing in the hall about their straight As, while we boys shoved our crumpled report cards deep into our backpacks. A guy might bemoan failing a stupid math test, but never would he brag about succeeding.

Likewise with reading. I remember one time I was watching *Jeopardy* with Cory and Bud. We were betting a dollar per question. It was a lot of money. I answered every question right and won about twenty bucks. "How the hell do you know all this shit?" Bud demanded. "You don't even watch TV."

"Reading, I guess."

"Get a life," Bud admonished. Then both of them clobbered me with the couch cushions.

But when I saw the low bookshelves in the corner of the taxidermy shed, I felt like I had a life, at least for the moment. If there was something decent, a novel or maybe a biography to read, I could stay the whole day. I rushed over even faster than I had toward the fridge. For weeks I hadn't encountered a book. Stacey didn't have a single one, just a couple of magazines about celebrities.

The titles were disappointing, though: *How to Paint Trout*, *The Complete Guide to Small Game*, *Turkey Taxidermy*, *How to Stuff a Skunk*, *Stuffed Animals and Pickled Heads*, *Taxing Taxidermy*, *Hunting the Wild Quail*. To name a few.

I picked up *Basic Taxidermy* and opened to the introduction. *Taxis* meant "movement," it told me, and *derma*, "skin." It then offered the advice that few recreational activities can equal the delight of rendering a dead animal back to its original condition. *Minus movement*, I thought. *Minus consciousness. Minus life. Like the deer. Like . . .*

I shoved the book back onto the shelf and went outside.

My clothes were getting dry, but only the outer edges of the pizza had thawed. The inside was as hard as a Popsicle. I gnawed at the doughy crust. It was pretty disgusting, but I didn't care. Just tasting the cheese and the icy tomato sauce made me ten times hungrier. I worked at the pizza until I had eaten half of it.

I spent the rest of the day paying for it. It reminded me of that scene in *Hatchet* where the kid eats all these berries at once. There was no bathroom, not even an outhouse, so I sat on a log, doubled over, hoping that no one would come along and surprise me.

When evening came and my stomach finally settled, I went into the shed and lay on the bear rug.

Every time I dozed off, I had that feeling of falling and jerked awake. Cory once told me that if you didn't wake up when you had that dream, you would die. I hoped it was true.

I woke up to a skittering sound. I wondered if the animals had come to life in the night. But this was a real one, a rodent racing across the floor, then back. It was smaller than my friend from the microwave—a mouse, I figured.

I didn't move. Soon it figured out what I already knew, that there was nothing to eat, and it scrambled off.

I tried to go back to sleep, but something kept edging me awake. Something important.

The pay phone.

The whole time I'd been at Stacey's, not once had I thought of using the phone. It was like I was paralyzed.

I grabbed the quarters and went outside. The moon seemed to shine directly on that square black box on the wall.

I stood in front of the phone and tried to remember Mira's number.

Nothing.

I was beginning to feel like one of those cases in that Oliver Sacks book *The Man who Mistook His Wife for a Hat.*

The book goes through all of these neurological cases where people have gaps in their thinking. One case was about a man who could only remember the absolute present. Another was about a guy whose brain sent the wrong signals about vision; he was the one who thought his wife was a hat.

I tried to remember my phone number, but I knew that was pointless. The only person who lived there any more was me, and I wasn't home.

Finally, a number popped into my head. I dropped four quarters into the phone and dialed it.

It was the supplier who sold us our books; an answering machine told me that the hours of business were between nine and four o'clock. I slammed down the phone. Only two of my quarters came back.

I waited. A cloud passed over the moon, darkening the sky. When I was little I thought the moon was a big eyeball because of the way it seemed to follow you when you moved.

Finally, another number came to life in my brain. The area code was unfamiliar; it definitely wasn't New England. I piled the quarters in.

"Hello."

I'd probably called her only a dozen times in my life, but that was the number I had in my mind, the one I probably needed most.

"Hello?" she said again. Margarite's voice. Alive. Present. My aunt.

Everything was solved. She could come and get me. We'd find my parents, then go home.

My voice rose into my throat. I tried to wrap it in my tongue, my teeth, the roof of my mouth, to make something out of it.

"Who is it?"

Nothing.

"Great!" she snarled. "A prank fucking phone call. Perfect timing, asshole." Then she stopped. She didn't slam down the phone like I thought she would.

She waited. I could hear her breathing. "Adam?" she ventured. "Adam, is it you?" She started to cry. She was bawling into the phone. "Goddamn it, Adam, you'd better be alive. If you're not, that's it. I'm telling you. That is fucking it."

A recording told me that my time was almost up.

"Adam!"

I pushed 9, then 3, then 7, to spell out *yes* on the number pad. Again and again. A Morse code of speechlessness. *Y-e-s. Yes, it's me. Adam. Alive.*

Then I was disconnected.

CHAPTER 20

compassion:
a feeling of pity that makes one want to help or show mercy.

When I woke up, I was completely disoriented. I heard water dripping and thought it was the coffeemaker at home. I smelled the must of mold and imagined I was on the wrestling mat.

I'd been dreaming about my aunt. I was walking down a pier. At the end of it were Margarite and Joey. They were holding poles that dangled colorful ribbons, beads, and ceramic animals. They were something Margarite carried in her shop. Dream catchers, she called them.

Joey turned toward me. Only instead of the blank, robotic expression he usually had, his face was lit up and smiling. "Adam!" He embraced me.

"He's cured!" I exclaimed to Margarite. "He can love."

"That's right." She turned to me, her expression blank, her voice mechanical. "I've changed places with him."

∧∕∨∕∨

I lay there a minute with my eyes closed, remembering the first time I met Margarite and Joey. We'd gone to visit her in South Carolina, on one of our few vacations. Joey was little, maybe two or three, but already you could tell there was something wrong. He didn't talk or make sounds. When Mom tried to hug him, he ducked her.

We'd brought him a big red fire truck. He took it off into a corner, but instead of playing with it, he turned it over, spun the wheels, and watched.

When it was time for dinner, Margarite pried him from the wheels, but he hardly ate a bite. Instead, he moved his food around on the plate, peas in a row, pieces of meat to the edges. "He doesn't like the foods to touch," Margarite mused. "Isn't that funny? But he's such an easy boy."

Mom said, "Yes. Very easy." But she looked really worried.

Margarite's husband was still with her then. His name was Chuck, and that's what Mom would say about him, in a whisper, to Dad. "He's a real *Chuck,* all right."

Chuck drank a lot of beer and watched TV. He was in the military and had one of those haircuts that looked like someone had driven a lawn mower over his head. He showed up to the table at meals, and Dad politely made conversation about sports while Mom and Margarite fussed over Joey.

∧∕∨∕∨

I opened my eyes and slowly got to my feet. In the morning light, the birds seemed friendlier, less like they were going to peck out my eyes.

The things I had taken for granted my whole life, a toothbrush, a cup of coffee, a comb, a meal, a shower, were nowhere to be found. I smoothed out my clothes as best as I could. I drank as much water from the faucet as I could handle, then headed out.

The ease with which I'd found the first couple of rides didn't last. Even with relatively clean clothes and hair, the cars sped past me like I was nothing.

Finally, a woman in a Mercedes stopped. Although she had dark hair, something about her reminded me of Mira's mom. Maybe it was just wealth: the giant ring on her hand, her diamond earrings. Or maybe it was the way she waved me to the backseat, dismissing me without even asking me where I was heading.

She was talking on a cell phone, one hand loosely on the wheel, as if she thought the car would drive itself.

I've never been a fan of cell phones. I have a hunch that people walk around with them glued to their ears just to give evidence that they have friends. Nobody in my family had one.

"Okay," she was saying into the phone, "maybe you should write this down. First, get a free-range duck. It has to be free-range. Of course they cost money. Free-range means they get to run around while they're alive, rather than being locked in a little pen always stepping in their own poop. Because it *tastes* better. Maybe it's the exercise. It sends flavor to the muscles or something. Whatever. What? No, that was the car door slamming. I just stopped to pick up a hitchhiker."

I could hear the male voice on the other side yelling.

"Calm down. Calm down." She peered at me in the rearview mirror. "He looks fine. He's just a teenager. Of course he's not armed. Are you armed?" she asked me.

I shook my head.

"See, he says he's not armed. No. No. He's fine. He was just standing on the road. What was I supposed to do? It's boiling out there. He'd have fried up like an egg on the sidewalk. It's a figure of speech. Right? I know they don't really fry. No. Look! My therapist said I should do more good deeds, give more, so I'll feel better about myself. Let's go back to the duck. Okay? I want it to be *l'orange*, so you need to get—no. No. Okay, I'll ask him. How far you going?"

I shrugged.

"He doesn't know. Not everybody is so focused on *destination* the way you are. Some are just there for the journey. I'll just drop him when I exit. He's fine. Well, he's tall, about six foot something. Blond hair in a ponytail. A ponytail! I don't know. Yes, he has long hair. I didn't notice until he got in and I saw the ponytail!" She was getting irritated. Picking me up was clearly causing her some major trouble. "Yeah. Actually, he is good-looking. Very handsome, although a little grubby. Maybe he's a college kid. Calm down. I'm old enough to be his mother. Stop! Okay. Okay. Just listen. Get some oranges, but make sure they're navel oranges. I don't want to have to pick out all the little seeds. And marsala. That's wine! Marsala is wine. Baby asparagus. You invited *her*? No, just that she's unbearable. Do you remember how she went on about Yoko Ono being *the* preeminent artist of the twentieth century. Absurd. No. He's just sitting there looking out the window. He doesn't seem to talk. Maybe he's foreign. Like, Swedish. Look, stop obsessing about the hitchhiker already." She clicked the phone off. "He is being so . . . difficult!"

A minute later, the phone rang. It rang to the tune of Beethoven's Fifth. Boy, did that fry my mom, that classical works of genius were being turned into ringer tunes. She also hated to see famous artwork in advertising or images of Einstein on T-shirts. "Is there anything that Americans won't commodify?" she'd gripe.

After the third call from her boyfriend or husband, the woman pulled onto the shoulder. "Sorry," she said, "he's gonna drive me crazy until I let you off. Really, he thinks you're an axe murderer. I guess it's sweet that he cares."

I nodded sympathetically. As I got out, she shoved a twenty at me. I had a feeling she probably solved a lot of her problems that way, with money. But that was cool with me; it was the first time I'd been paid in a while.

CHAPTER 21

embody:
to express principles or ideas in a visible form

Once I started the motion toward home, it was all I could think about. I had ten rides in three days, made my way across Arkansas, Tennessee, and North Carolina with ease. It was nothing like the trip I'd had with my parents, where we'd taken side roads through towns and eaten at local places. This time, I saw nothing. I clung to the highways, where every place looked the same: McDonalds, Burger King, Comfort Inn. I spent the twenty on snacks and drinks in gas stations and diners, a comb, a razor, and a pair of scissors to cut my hair.

People separate themselves from each other by so many things: race, gender, religion, class. But on my travels, I learned to distinguish people by the only thing that really matters: kindness. There were people who drove past me yelling obscenities out the window, or who acted like they were going to run over me, then swerved at the last minute. There were those who picked me up grudgingly, like someone had told them they had to do a good deed to get into heaven, or who pretended that I was the silent psychotherapist and they could vent about everything they hated in this world and would hate in the next. Then there were the kind ones: a family on the way to a reunion, who fed me tuna sandwiches, cake, and soda from a cooler; a man who tried to get me to write my destination so he could take me the whole way, then waited and watched after he dropped me to make sure I got another ride; an old man who let me stay in his motel room with him, then bought me breakfast.

I did my share of walking, too. I must have walked at least fifty miles. The soles of my shoes came loose and flapped like the mouths of puppets. I didn't care. I was heading toward home.

But then, in Virginia, my progress came to a halt, and I got stuck.

The weather was terrible, rain blasting down in sheets. I ducked into an Exxon station and camped out in the bathroom for a night. The next morning, I stood at the highway entrance in the rain for hours without anyone stopping.

A feeling kept rising in me; it was not familiar. Anger. Rage. If I'd had a BB gun, I would have shot at the tires of the cars that passed me. I remembered a book I'd read about the stages of death. One stage was denial. Another was rage. I couldn't remember the rest, but it didn't matter. Whatever they were, I was stuck at rage.

Finally, a van pulled up. The driver was a woman, but something was off with her. She looked the way Bud did after he started using crystal meth: her face twitchy, her eyes bugging out. "Get in," she commanded.

My mom always taught me to pay attention to my feelings. "Go with your gut," she always said.

I peered at the woman's crazy expression, and my stomach went into knots.

"Come on, honey," she coaxed. "I'm not gonna bite you."

From the back of the van, I heard a guy cackling. "Get in, asshole."

I backed off and ran. It really freaked me out. I stopped hitching for the day and walked toward the tall buildings of downtown, then wandered the streets of Richmond like a zombie. By then, my twenty was spent, and I hadn't showered in days; I must have looked pretty bad. When a woman saw me standing, dazed, at a street corner, she reached into her pocket and handed me a quarter.

This is how it happens, I thought, *that people become homeless.* One thing goes wrong, then another, and then everything unravels, like pulling a thread and having the cloth come apart in your hands.

That night I slept in a Dumpster.

The level of my hunger pissed me off. It was like this problem I would solve over and over again, but which always came back. I was walking back and forth past a row of restaurants, trying to get up the nerve to run in and grab some food when I passed an alley and saw a man in a white apron emptying out trays into the dumpster. When he went back inside, I went over to check it out. Luckily, the food had landed on a stack of flattened boxes. Scrambled eggs and sausages.

I climbed inside. The eggs were cold, but good. The sausages were hard as sticks. They made me gag as they went down.

The Dumpster wasn't all that bad, though. It was protected by an overhang from the rain. The boxes made pretty good covers, even if I did wake up with scrambled eggs in my hair.

It was one of the low points of my travels, but not the lowest. It just felt like I was going to end up there forever, a bum in the South, maybe the youngest bum in town.

CHAPTER 22

radius:
1. a straight line extending from the center of a circle or sphere to its circumference.

My third day in Richmond, the rain stopped coming down. Instead it rose into the air as humidity, sticky as sweat. No food had appeared in the Dumpster that morning, so I climbed out and made my way to the streets.

I knew I had to go back to the highway, to stick my thumb out into the air and let the fates have me, but I was still feeling spooked about hitching. So I walked around trying to find something other than a gumball that I could buy with a quarter. I passed a barber, a magic shop with a lit-up rabbit popping out of a top hat, and a coin shop where two men outside were going on and on about the Yankees. It took me a couple of minutes to realize they were talking about northerners and not baseball.

I saw a shelter that offered meals, but when I got closer, I saw that it was boarded up. I checked a phone booth, but local calls were thirty-five cents, and the receiver was missing from the cord anyway. I passed a bookstore called Virginia's Woolves. I wanted to go in there so badly, but I was afraid that if I went in, I would fall to pieces. And I didn't need that. Not now. I was on my way home.

"There are three kinds of luck," my dad used to say: "good luck, bad luck, and no luck at all." Dad loved to play penny poker. He bought lottery tickets and planned how we'd spend the money when he won (travel around the world for a year, then set up a foundation for charity). But he considered himself in the bad luck category. He said that was why he'd been distracted by a baby crying and got knocked out in the first round of the Newark championship, why he'd busted his wrist chopping wood for a neighbor just before his most important boxing match. "The only real luck I've had," he once said, "is you and your mom."

I had barely started hitching that day when I had my first piece of good luck. A couple of kids in a beat-up Volvo stopped.

They looked pretty much alike. Both had red hair, although the younger kid had a wide face and slanted eyes. He looked like he had Down's syndrome. I figured they were brothers.

To the usual question, where I was going, I pointed up, my way of indicating north.

"We're headed toward Arlington," the driver said.

Arlington was close to D.C., I knew. I got in the backseat.

"I'm Chad and this is Sandy," the older brother said. He pulled onto the highway. I waved. Sandy turned around and looked at me. "Who are you?"

I made a gesture to say I didn't talk.

"Are you deaf?"

I shook my head.

"I have deaf friends," he offered. "They talk with their hands. You should learn to do that."

"Buckle your seat belt, Sandy," his brother scolded. "You always forget."

"Where are we going in Arlington?" Sandy asked his brother. It was like it was the first time it occurred to him that there was a destination.

"I told you."

"You didn't."

"Twin Meadows."

"I don't wanna go to Twin Meadows," Sandy complained. "It's not nice there."

"It's very nice."

"I wanna go to the mall. The mall is on the way."

"We're going to Twin Meadows. Remember? There's a picnic today."

"Mall! I want a soft pretzel."

"There'll be lots of good food at the picnic: fried chicken and potato salad, cakes and pies. You like cakes and pies."

My mouth watered.

"No, I don't. I like soft pretzels."

"Dad is going to be there too."

"I wanna get new shoes."

"You have new shoes."

"I don't like these shoes."

"You wanted those shoes. You begged for those shoes."

"They looked better in the catalog."

"Too bad."

"They don't fit."

"I told you to try them on before you wore them outside. If you'd done that, we could've returned them."

"I want to get new shoes at the mall," Sandy insisted.

The arguing went on for the next twenty minutes, Sandy demanding that they stop at the mall, ride the carousel, buy shoes, eat a pretzel, and look in the shop with the windup toys.

Just keep driving, I thought.

As we approached the mall, though, Chad pulled off the highway.

"Yay!" Sandy cheered.

"I'm not going to the mall." Chad pulled into the parking lot. "I'm letting you off here. I can't stand any more of your nagging. I've had it. See that bus stop? The blue line goes to Twin Meadows. I'm going to put you on that bus and you can go there by yourself."

"But the bus costs quarters. I don't have quarters."

"No," Chad said maliciously. "The blue line is free, because it's the one the retards ride. Like you!"

Sandy started to cry. "I'm not a retard. I just wanted new shoes, nice shoes for the picnic. These shoes are too tight. And a good soft pretzel with cheese sauce."

"I don't have money for new shoes." Chad sighed. I could tell the crying made him lose his resolve. "Tell you what—we'll go in and get the pretzel. That's all. Twenty minutes. No more. Then we're going to Twin Meadows."

His brother clapped his hands. "Goody!"

"Fine." Chad pulled into a parking space, hopped out, and opened my door. I was hoping I could go into the mall, too, and then continue on with them, but he pointed across the parking lot. "Just cross the street and you'll be back at the highway." He strode off.

"I always get my way." Sandy winked at me, then tagged after his brother and grabbed his hand. They disappeared between the cars.

I was walking toward the exit when I saw the bus stop for the blue line. It was free and it went to Twin Meadows, Chad had told his brother. And I knew one important thing about Twin Meadows: There was a picnic.

CHAPTER 23

dissociate:
to separate in one's thoughts.

My dad's favorite boxer was Joe Louis. Maybe it was because Louis became a symbolic hero in 1938, when he fought the German champion, Schmeling. Louis beat Schmeling in just over two minutes, giving the whole country the idea that Hitler could also be beaten that easily. His second favorite was Rocky Marciano. Both Louis and Marciano were quick on their feet, something Dad was not. Dad was big, too tall to move the way a boxer needed to.

Dad knew all the great fights by heart, round by round, and the boxers' life stories. He knew that when Marciano beat Louis, he cried in his dressing room, because Louis had been his hero. He knew that Louis died poor and Marciano died young, in a plane crash. Both boxers had been as kind and nonviolent in life as they had been violent in the ring. That was important to Dad. He couldn't stand the boxers who beat their wives or picked fights outside the ring.

Needless to say, he wasn't a big fan of Mike Tyson. To Dad, boxing was a noble sport, one that should not be disgraced in private life.

The blue-line bus pulled up to the stop. I sure hoped it was air-conditioned. I'd never been in the South before, but I knew I wouldn't be back if I could help it; it was like moving through hot soup.

When the doors opened, I hesitated. Maybe Chad was lying to Sandy about it being free. I only had one quarter. The bus driver examined me as I hopped on, but he didn't complain when I moved to a seat without paying.

As we drove, I watched out the window, carefully. I figured I'd take the bus back to the mall after the picnic, but just in case, I wanted to keep my bearings.

The bus was cool, a relief. I had the beginning of a wicked headache. I didn't know if it was hunger or if I was getting sick.

At the next stop, two women with giant shopping bags shoved in. I noticed that they both dropped coins into the slot. Maybe it was only us "retards" who didn't have to pay.

One of the women was pregnant. I stood up to offer my seat.

"There are other seats," she snapped, as if I had insulted her. I'd never experienced the effect of how you look on others. If I'd been my regular self, showered, in clean clothes with a real haircut, the lady probably would have thanked me for offering my seat.

"Did you check the sex of the baby?" I heard the woman's friend ask from the seats they'd taken behind me.

"I didn't want to, but Ricky insisted, and I didn't want him to know and me to not know."

"Well, it's easier for the shower."

"True, but I think there's something sacrilegious about it. I mean, the whole of human history, people have had to guess, to *intuit* the sex of a baby. In Africa, certain tribes will slaughter a lion; if the entrails drip out to the north, it's a girl, and if they drip out to the south, it's a boy."

"What if they drip east or west?"

"They don't."

"Why not?"

"They just don't." She sounded irritated. "Geography, I guess."

"I don't think that story's true. I mean . . . it's not that easy to slaughter a lion. It's not like a rabbit or a cow. A lion is very likely to slaughter you first. Besides, how could they come up with that many lions, anyway? I mean, lions aren't a dime a dozen."

"The *National Geographic* doesn't lie."

"Maybe you were reading *The National Enquirer*."

"Oh, you're impossible."

"That's what my husband tells me." The woman laughed.

I liked her a lot more than the pregnant one. "So what is it?"

"What is what?"

"The baby!"

"A boy."

"Rick must be thrilled."

"Well . . . he is, except he said something funny."

"What?"

"He said, 'Too bad. If it was a girl, she'd get a free ride like you.'"

"Uh-oh."

"It's part of his antifeminist stuff, I think. Don't you? I mean, he thinks pregnancy is a big scam, just because I quit my job."

"What are you going to name him?"

"Rufus!"

"You're kidding?"

"After this dog I had when I was a kid. Every morning, rain or shine, the dog would come and lick my face. And if I lost something, like a baby doll or a book, I would tell him and he would find it."

"Twin Meadows," the bus driver called out.

Two guys got off the bus ahead of me. One of them was limping. The other waddled along like a duck. I wondered what I was in for, but I followed them up the street until a wooden sign appeared: TWIN MEADOWS.

I had pictured green pastures flanking a nice pond,

maybe, or endless fields of wildflowers. But the "meadows" were two patches of dried grass flanking a crumbling side- walk. At the end of it was a massive brick house that looked like it could topple at any second. A wrought-iron fence sur- rounded the whole place.

I walked around the periphery of the fence. I didn't want any problems; if I got in, I wanted to make sure I'd get out. But then I noticed that the gates at the back, by the parking lot, were open. At least for today, people could come and go.

Hanging on the fence was a set of green scrubs, like the kind doctors wear in hospitals. I picked up the scrubs and walked toward the parking lot.

As I got closer to the building, I could see a canopy and long tables: the picnic. There were several young men play- ing horseshoes on the grass. A couple of them looked like Sandy, like they had Down's syndrome. There was a woman with a head the size of my fist carrying a red-tipped cane, and a man flapping his hands who reminded me of Joey. All of them were wearing the green scrubs.

I pulled the scrubs over my clothes. They were short, but otherwise they fit. Then I snuck through the parking lot and onto the lawn.

There were two or three people in white—nurses, I guessed. Others, in street clothes, were starting to arrive. I hadn't needed the scrubs after all. I watched for Chad and Sandy. I figured I'd better beat it if they came.

A nurse walked over to the table and pulled the covers off the food. When she left, I moved to the table and grabbed a plate.

There was fried chicken, potato salad, macaroni and cheese, beets, sliced tomatoes, okra, rice pudding, and Jell-O. I piled food on my plate, poured a large iced tea, and snuck off to the farthest corner of the lawn.

I was shoveling the food in as fast as I could, when a girl on crutches struggled over. She was in green, and she spoke as if her tongue was swollen against her teeth, but at least she spoke. She had one up on me.

"You weren't supposed to eat until *all* the visitors were here," she scolded. "You're not using good manners. I'm gonna tell."

I made a pleading gesture.

"Give me one reason why I shouldn't. Because you're cute? I don't care if you're cute. I'm immune to boys. Boys are tough. They cause trouble. They don't follow the rules."

I offered her a piece of bread and butter.

"I don't want your food. That's dirty food. And you're dirty." She started to head off, but then she stopped, and pointed across the lawn. "Naakkkked."

A naked man was running across the lawn, back and forth as if he were practicing for a race.

"Alan!" one of the nurses shouted. "Stop right there!"

But Alan didn't stop. He kept running with complete abandon, his legs high, his arms pumping. And I knew by his size that he was naked because his clothes had disappeared—and I was wearing them.

One of the male nurses took chase. The two of them circled the picnic table. Then, as the nurse got closer, naked Alan made a dive for the table, his body sliding across the bowls of food, knocking them off the table. I was really glad I'd already eaten.

I shed the scrubs and dropped them on the chair, then dashed toward the parking lot. "He melted!" I heard my friend exclaim.

I was almost out of the parking lot when I had my best piece of luck. A Honda Accord was parked in the fire lane, the engine running, the windows down. I opened the door of the car, slid in, adjusted the seat and mirrors, and put the car in drive.

In a few minutes, I was back at the mall. I fumbled for the turn signal, changed lanes, and slid onto the highway. WASHINGTON D.C., a sign said. Thirty-six miles.

I was about six or seven hours from home. I felt like driving a hundred miles per hour just to get there faster. But I kept my desire in check and leveled at sixty-five. I didn't want to call attention to myself. I was driving a stolen car.

CHAPTER 24

rebellion:
open resistance to authority, especially organized armed resistance to an established government.

Driving the highway, I thought about how I had changed, and not for the better. Not that I was a total goody two-shoes before or anything. Like I said, I did my share of pranks, got drunk a few times, entered into a sexual relationship after promising my parents I'd wait until I was eighteen. I was far from perfect, but still, this was the first time I'd committed a felony.

I guess anyone who reads a lot knows that most people are capable of every kind of behavior given a certain set of circumstances. Like the boys in *Lord of the Flies* who become savages and murder Simon and Piggy. Or Raskolnikov in *Crime and Punishment,* who murders a pawnbroker and her half sister in order to help a poor family.

Ethics are slipperier than most people think. I had to remember that before I judged someone. My mom and dad weren't religious. "Most of the bad stuff that goes on in the

world happens in the name of God. You ever notice that?"
Mom said, when I asked her why we didn't go to church like
other families I knew.

But she had a phrase that she used quite often: "There,
but for the grace of God, go I." She meant, don't judge
people. Their plight could be yours. Their bad luck.

As I got closer to D.C., the number of cop cars multiplied. It
made me pretty nervous. Once, I even saw blue flashing
lights behind me, but the cop sped past. I hoped the car's
owner was still at the picnic, scarfing down fried chicken or
whatever else was left over after Alan's table dive, rather than
dropping someone off and returning to their car. I hoped
the E-Zpass that would get me through tolls wouldn't tell it
was a stolen car.

I hit the radio. It was on an AM station. A baseball player
was talking about winning the World Series. "Man," he said.
"I was the man. I mean, we were all the man that night."

I flipped to FM and rolled down the window. America
flew past me. I was on my way.

An old Al Green song came on that made me think of
Mira. *I am so in love with you. Whatever you want to do is all
right with me.*

For several nights after Mira asked me to make love with
her, I couldn't sleep. It was as if the possibility of that ever

happening had been locked in a little closet, and now the door had popped open.

I paced my room, looking out the window like the sky would give an answer. I could practically feel our bodies next to each other. It was all I could think about.

But it wasn't just sex. So many of the guys had sex with girls just to do it, but I didn't want it to be that way. I felt like if I did that my first time, the experience would be empty forever. With Mira, I wanted it to be something special, almost sacred. To make us closer. And I knew that she would be my first, and maybe even my last. That's how strongly I felt about her.

We had a couple of books on sex at our shop. They were actually written for gay women on how to please each other. I peeked at them when my parents were out, studied the illustrations of which parts of women's bodies gave them pleasure. It sounds kind of stupid now, but that was my habit in life. You want to know about something, or how to do something? Get a book.

The next step was to buy condoms. Everyone knows me and my parents in town, so I didn't go to the local pharmacy. Instead, I drove over the Mt. Hope Bridge to Portsmouth and went to CVS. I bought a bunch of other stuff—shaving cream and candy—to make the condoms less noticeable. Still, my hands were shaking as I placed the package on the checkout stand and watched it move toward the checker on the belt.

She was a middle-aged lady, with black hair and heavy makeup. She reminded me of Elvira, Mistress of the Dark, who hosted scary movies on TV. She rang it up without comment. Then, as I pulled out my wallet, she looked at me, narrowed her eyes, and said, "God, I need a cigarette." That was it.

With every mile, I got more elated, more excited, even though I was starting to feel seriously lousy: my throat aching, my head throbbing.

But as I crossed from Delaware into New Jersey, my luck changed. The car started to sputter. I looked at the gas gauge. The needle was on empty, all the way at the end of the red light. I needed to get off the highway. There was no way I'd catch a ride on it; the cars were going too fast.

By the time I coasted down the off-ramp, the car had stalled completely. I managed to pull it onto the shoulder and hop out. I checked the car to see if there was anything that would help me. It was something I should have done in Idaho: taken what I needed, like a bottle of water, like my wallet.

There was nothing there. Just a flier that announced the picnic. It reminded me that at least I wasn't hungry. I grabbed the sheet of paper and ran off the exit.

It took me about forty minutes to find the on-ramp. Then I pulled out the marker I'd taken from the taxidermy shed and pulled off the cap.

Write, I instructed myself. *Words.*

At home, I had about twenty journals. My dad gave us each a new journal every New Year's Day. He wrote poems in his. Mom kept hers secret. I filled mine with stuff about my day: the wrestling scores, funny things Mira said, parties I went to, weird dreams, ideas for papers. Writing was as natural to me as reading or speaking.

Come on, I coaxed myself. It was like trying to remember the phone numbers. My mind wouldn't cooperate with me.

Goddamn it, write! I demanded.

Words are power. It's corny, I know, but my silence had taught me that much. You're nothing if you can't communicate.

My hand shook and wobbled like a little kid's as I pressed the marker to the paper. Then I wrote, in big, dark block letters, the two words that meant more to me than anything at that moment: *RHODE ISLAND.*

CHAPTER 25

counterbalance:
a weight or influence that balances another

I held up my sign at the highway entrance. I hoped I was doing the right thing. I mean, there were probably people who might have picked me up but didn't because they weren't going that far. I was in a hurry, too. At any second I expected the police to pull up and arrest me for stealing the car.

About an hour passed, but it felt like ten. I felt so weak, it was hard to hold up the sign. I was about to walk off the ramp when a car slowed, then pulled into the breakdown lane.

My heart beat wildly. My luck was back. The car had Rhode Island plates.

A woman was driving. She wore a black turtleneck and had equally black circles under her eyes.

"Do something." She motioned to the backseat, where a little boy was screaming and crying.

I waved at the little boy. He kicked the back of his mom's

seat and howled louder. I got in and slipped on my seat belt. The mother tore back onto the road.

The boy looked like he was about three. My mom volunteered at the Head Start program. A couple of times I'd gone with her. He reminded me of those kids: a runny nose, pale skin like he didn't play enough out in the sun.

The mom looked at me in the mirror. "This is the last time I ever go to someone's wedding out of state. They're so depressing, anyway. The wife-to-be was very clearly flirting with the best man. My cousin, the groom, was half in the bag as usual."

I nodded to let her know I was listening; then I turned my attention to the screaming kid.

I played peekaboo. He screamed. I made funny faces. He kicked the back of her seat. I was afraid that if I couldn't calm him down, the mom would kick *me* out of the car.

I searched around. There were the remnants of a popped balloon, some empty Coke cans, a top, and a roll of kite string.

I spun the string on the front of his car seat. He swatted it away and howled even louder.

Next, I worked at the kite string until it tore off. Then I knotted it and shaped it into a cat's cradle. But instead of offering it to him, I played with it by myself.

After a couple of seconds, his crying slowed down and he watched. Then he held up his hands like mine. I made an arc of string on his fingers, then looped it away from him.

He giggled, then reached back for it.

"A miracle," the mom sighed. "Where are you going in Rhode Island?"

I made waves with my hands.

"The coast?"

I nodded.

"South County?"

No.

"Newport?"

Closer.

"Imagine! You standing there with your Rhode Island sign. I would never have picked you up if it wasn't for that sign. I thought, 'Well, I'll take my chances.' I'm going to Middletown," she said. "If we're lucky we'll make it by midnight. I'll drop you there. Okay?"

Middletown was about ten miles from where I lived. *A miracle,* I thought. *Yes.*

CHAPTER 26

**imbroglio:
a confused situation, usually involving a disagreement.**

The more I played cat's cradle, the blurrier my eyes became. My stomach was whirling. My throat was as sore as any scraped knee. My face felt hot.

The little boy had no mercy, though. Even when it got dark, he insisted we exchange the geometric strings. I felt like jumping out of the car.

Finally, in Connecticut, the mom swerved off the highway and pulled into the drive-thru at a McDonald's.

The food wars with my mom were very much like the boxing and wrestling wars: minor and easily won. My mom was not only a vegetarian, she was opposed to the corporate takeover of America, the homogenization of just about everything. Wal-Mart was first on her list of public enemies. They closed down independently owned businesses, outsourced, paid low wages, and kept employee hours just low enough so they wouldn't have to pay benefits. McDonald's was second. She grudgingly admitted that they had a better record than Wal-Mart, but she was miffed that McDonald's epitomized American culture to much of the world. "How can a slice of gray meat on a bun with ketchup become a cultural icon?"

In high school, once I had friends who drove, I got pretty attached to Big Macs and the greasy, salty strips that passed for french fries. It was one of the things I bought with my paychecks.

My mom tried to forbid me, but Dad took my side. "It's his money and he works hard for it," he said. "Besides, most parents are concerned about drugs and alcohol, not burgers."

Mom snorted. "Just don't let me see the empty bags."

"Bring me some too," Dad whispered.

"I heard that." Mom tackled him.

The kid was clapping his hands. "Hap-hap-happy Meal!"

I'd finally get a break from cat's cradle. I leaned my head against the window. It felt like ice on my skin.

"Cheeseburger and milk, Sam?"

So I finally knew his name.

"Coke!" Sam shouted.

"No Coke!"

"I want Coke!"

"Want anything?" she asked me.

I patted my pocket, just to be sure, although I knew

there was no money there. The mom hadn't told me her story the way some of my rides did, but I could tell by the split upholstery of the car that she wasn't Donald Trump. I shook my head.

"Sure?"

I nodded.

"Happy Meal," she said to the speaker, "with a cheeseburger and milk, no pickle, apple pie, and a large coffee."

Water, I thought. That was what I needed. I was dying of thirst and it was free. I tapped her shoulder, mimed drinking.

"Coke?" she asked. "Sprite? Coffee?" Finally, she got it.

"And a small water," she called out.

Not small, I thought. My thirst felt unquenchable. I knew from sports that when you got dehydrated, you had all the symptoms I felt: nausea, chills, dizziness.

"Potty, Sam? Gotta go potty?"

"No!"

"You?" she asked. I could have gone. It wasn't a bad idea, but I was so scared she'd change her mind and drive off without me that I shook my head. No way was I losing this ride.

She paid and passed the food back. "He doesn't like ketchup on his fries," she instructed. "Please make sure there's no pickle. They make him throw up."

I drank the water in one gulp, then opened Sam's meal. When I tried to pass the fries, he swatted them so that most of them spilled on the floor of the car: "Toy, toy," he chanted.

I opened the toy. It was the donkey from the movie *Shrek*. William Steig, who wrote *Shrek*, was Mom's favorite kids' author. She'd read me all of his books when I was little: *Brave Irene*, about the girl who carries a dress through a snowstorm for her sick mother; *Yellow & Pink*, about the existence of God; *Sylvester and the Magic Pebble*, about a donkey who turns into a stone and whose parents pine for him. Most of Steig's books were about family love and devotion, and Steig never talked down to the reader. Mom would have hated to see the movie toys, just as she hated the books from the movie that showed up after Steig died. The only time I saw her be rude to a customer was when some lady complained that we didn't have *Rugrats* books. "Maybe your son would like to read a book rather than a TV show," Mom snapped.

Sam made animated little voices, then whacked the donkey against his car seat. "Donkey off the cliff." He shoved the donkey onto the floor. As I bent to retrieve it, I shoved the fallen french fries into my mouth.

When he got tired of getting rid of the donkey, he demanded his food. "Booger! Booger!"

I unwrapped it, checked for pickles, and handed it to him, hoping he wouldn't finish it.

"You're a good helper." The mom smiled in the rearview

mirror. "It's lucky I picked you up, although I was very nervous about it."

I smiled. I'd take any compliment I could get.

Sam gobbled the whole thing down. I wondered if he'd even chewed. I felt like I was going to cry.

The more we drove, the worse I felt. They say, "the room is spinning," but cars spin even more. The french fries I'd eaten off the floor didn't help.

"Is he asleep?" The mom eyed me in the mirror.

I glanced over at Sam. To my surprise, he was.

I nodded.

"Thank God," his mom said.

I took Sam's blanket and covered him.

Yes, I thought. *Thank God.*

She turned on the radio. An old Sting song was playing: "Fragile."

On and on the rain will fall, like tears from a star. On and on the rain will say, how fragile we are.

Fragile. Yeah. Everything was. Even the lines on the road were broken into white gashes, like the scars on Mira's arms.

CHAPTER 27

celestial:
1. of the sky. 2. of heaven, divine.

The day Mira and I finally made love was months after the scene in her bedroom. We were on a school trip to Maine, in a town called Blue Hill that was full of bakeries, galleries, and bookstores. I love Maine. The people in Maine aren't afraid to be characters, to be themselves. There's nothing homogenized about them. Maybe it has something to do with surviving those freezing winters.

People say the coast of Maine is rocky, and it is, but there are also these gentle coves and mud flats that, in low tide, go out forever. Mira and I had snuck away from the group and waded out across to this massive stone, an island in the water. One side of it jutted up like the back of a couch. It gave us complete privacy.

There was something about being away from home, even if it was with the school, that made me feel relaxed and open. The ocean, too, has always given me a limitless feeling.

I grew up on it, and I knew I'd never move anywhere where I couldn't smell salt in the air.

Mira sat cross-legged and looked up at me. It reminded me of the way she looked the day she came in the bookstore for the first time. So serious and deep. I bent to kiss her, and she pulled me down, laughing, then I was touching her everywhere.

The condom in my wallet was flat from waiting, but it worked. The instructions I had read in the books about sex flew out of my head. Our bodies became like water. The corny thing that people always say about love came into my mind: that you're one person; that you *become* one person. It was the most awesome experience I'd ever had.

After, we lay on the stone, our eyes closed. I fell asleep a little. Then, suddenly, Mira gave me a shove. I sat up with a start.

She was pointing at the mud flat we'd come out on, or at what used to be the mud flat. The water had risen so that the path we'd crossed was erased. The stone itself was disappearing rapidly in the flood of the rising tide. "Holy shit— we are in for it!" she said.

The tide was actually pretty strong, and the water was too deep for me to reach the bottom, but we were both decent swimmers; we made it to shore. When we got there, though, our class was nowhere in sight. The place where they'd been peering at fossils was underwater. They'd retreated as the tide rose.

It took us a couple of hours to find them, or rather for them to find us. They'd moved into the woods to search for mushrooms—or what our teacher, Bergeson, called "forest floor fungi"—before they realized we were missing. A couple of the kids made crude comments, I later found out. Bergeson told them to shut up; then a search ensued.

Mira came up with a quick story about her wallet falling out of her pocket, then floating off in the rising water. "Thank goodness Adam helped me swim out after it!" she exclaimed. It was about as lame as lame could get. There were plenty of snickers.

"Well, that's just odd enough to be true." Bergeson glared at them. But I could tell from his expression that he knew exactly what we'd been doing. My red face probably gave us away.

Mira and I got to carry all the equipment for the rest of the trip, and Bergeson started sleeping in my tent with me. He snored like crazy.

I woke up to Sam's voice. He was talking in his sleep about the donkey taking his blanket.

Then my eyes beheld a beautiful sight: the Newport Bridge, rising above Narragansett Bay like the curved wings of a giant, ascending bird. And the wings were lit up by what we locals call a necklace of lights.

I wondered if I'd now be able to speak. It seemed only right that I should. That everything should return to me: my voice, my senses, my *sense*. But when I opened my mouth, all I could feel was the agony in my throat.

"We're almost home," Sam's mom said. "Thank God. I never want to leave this state again as long as I live."

I couldn't have agreed with her more.

CHAPTER 28

discern:
to perceive clearly with the mind or senses.

She left me in a parking lot in Middletown. "There'll be a phone in the bar," she instructed. "You can call a cab from there."

That would be nice, I thought. *Call a cab.* If I had money or a voice.

I gave Sam one last look. He was still sleeping in his car seat, looking angelic. His mom would lift him like that, carry him into the house, his room. She'd lay him carefully on the bed and tuck him in.

He didn't know how good he had it.

The smart thing would have been to get a decent night's sleep somewhere, find a motel or an abandoned building to sneak into, then set out in the morning. But there was only the bar.

I walked toward the entrance. Music poured out of it like smoke. The dirty-socks smell of stale beer. There was a stool there for the bouncer, but it was empty. I went inside. A sign announced the "Saturday Special," a double Pina Colada. Was it still Saturday? It was the longest day of my life.

The place was packed.

The loud disco music made the walls thud. Or maybe it was my head. A singer belted out that she would survive; as long as she knew how to love, she'd stay alive. I tried to remember the singer's name. I listened to people's conversations, trying to catch the Rhode Island accent, a poor stepchild of the Massachusetts drawl: *Pahk the cah.* Just to make sure I was really here.

I was dying of thirst. I searched for leftover drinks. I drank the watery end of a Coke, a flat beer, then something that tasted like bourbon or scotch. I went to the bathroom, then moved through the crowded bar just to feel the warm bodies brush against me. I stood at the edge of the dance floor and watched people dance.

Home. I couldn't stop saying it in my mind. *Almost home.* Close enough. If I could hitch a ride the last few miles, I'd be there.

"In a good book, the hero or heroine meets obstacles, but they are overcome by the character, by his or her own effort," Ms. Ross used to say. I'd done that. And now I didn't want to have to overcome anything. I wanted someone to take over now, to take care of everything. I wanted to be five, or two, a baby left on a doorstep. A child.

I must be pretty sick, I thought. The room felt like one of those jumping castles. My throat raged. It reminded me of the one time I had strep and couldn't swallow. My mom had to give me a wet cloth to put in my mouth to absorb the saliva. I stayed home from school for the whole week.

I felt dizzy and stumbled backward, bumping into a kid wearing a cowboy hat and boots. No one wears cowboy boots in New England. It reminded me of Idaho, of Rad. "Watch out. You made me spill my beer," he slurred.

I held up my hands, an apology.

"Jerk!" He sounded drunk. I turned to go, but he grabbed me from behind. Why did these guys always wait until your back was turned? It was a cliché, but it was true.

I was trying to just shake him off. But he stumbled and fell against someone's table.

I didn't stick around to hear the people at the table get pissed off. I turned and made my way outside.

CHAPTER 29

irony:
1. the expression of one's meaning by using words of the opposite meaning in order to make one's remarks forceful. 2. (of an occurrence) the quality of being so unexpected or ill-timed that it appears to be deliberately perverse.

I should have kept walking and followed my dad's rule: "Go the other direction from trouble."

But I didn't. The parking lot was lit up and full of cars. The road was dark and I wasn't sure where I was.

Two guys were leaning against a white pickup truck in the parking lot. One of them was extremely thin and tall; the other was short and fat.

"Come on," the thin one argued. "Let's hit Dicey's."

"That joint in Portsmouth?"

"Yeah, it's open till two."

"I don't want to miss Jay Leno. It probably already started."

To hear them mention Portsmouth thrilled me. It was

the next town over from my town. I walked over and pointed to the bed of the truck.

"What?" the thin guy asked. "You want a ride?"

I nodded.

The chubby guy had a rubbery face, or maybe my vision was blurred. But something about his expression gave me a tug of doubt. I ignored it.

"You don't have to sit back there. We can squeeze you in." The skinny kid opened the door, then went around to the driver's side. I got in. Then the other one got in next to me, wedging me into the middle.

The driver started the engine and reversed.

"Hey, wait for Thomas," the chubby guy said.

"Where the hell is he?"

"I don't know. He disappeared onto the dance floor like an hour ago with some babe."

"She was a dog."

"What's your name?" the chubby one asked.

I pointed to my throat.

"What?" the skinny one said. "Laryngitis?"

I nodded.

"I'm Larry," the chubby one offered.

"And I'm Moe," the thin one joked.

"See. We're the Three Stooges. And here comes Curly."

It was the kid with the cowboy hat. When I saw him, I tried to get out of the cab, but things happened too fast.

Larry jumped into the small backseat so Curly could squeeze in. Curly slammed the door, and Moe tore out of the parking lot.

It took a second for Curly to notice me. "Well," Curly slurred. "Just look what the cat drug in."

CHAPTER 30

cauterize:
to burn the surface (of living tissue) with a caustic or a
hot iron in order to destroy infection or stop bleeding.

For a couple of minutes, no one said anything. I watched carefully as we drove. We were on back roads, heading into Portsmouth, but it was farm country. There were no streetlights. It was hard to figure out where we were.

"Shit, I'm hungry," Moe said. "Is anything open?"

I got hopeful. If they stopped for food, I could get out.

"Nothing is open after midnight in this stupid state."

"What about Dicey's?" Moe suggested.

"They don't serve food," Larry said.

"I have a peanut-butter sandwich somewhere. Thomas," Moe accused, "you're stepping on my sandwich."

Curly looked under his foot at the squashed, flat sandwich. "It's a pancake."

"I don't care. My blood sugar's going ape shit. I want my sandwich."

"What? Did your *mommy* make it?"

"As a matter of fact, yes."

Curly passed the sandwich across me to Moe. "Mama's boy."

"Wanna bite?" Moe asked Larry.

"Hell, no."

"You?" Moe offered it to me.

I felt like crying at Moe's kindness. Despite my hunger, I shook my head.

"Remember in second grade, that kid Sherman was allergic to peanuts?" Larry said.

"Yeah," Moe agreed. "And he was always going on about it in class, like if a mom brought in cupcakes for someone's birthday, Sherman would be like . . ."

"'Miss Corey, if there's peanuts in there, I could die.'" They said it together.

"Yeah, he was annoying," Moe said.

"Then one day, we're in the cafeteria and they're serving like chicken chow mein. They're trying to be 'multicultural' or some shit, and Sherman takes a bite of this other kid's chow mein. I guess there was, like, peanut oil in it."

"Oh, man. I'd forgotten about that."

"So what happened?" Curly asked. I guess he hadn't gone to school with them.

"He turns bright red, and his face swells up. He's gagging for breath, and all of us are just, like, watching him, because it was kind of cool—"

"But also scary."

"Yeah. His eyes are swelling up and everything, and he's gasping. Finally, the teacher comes rushing over, and then the nurse. The nurse has this shot in her hand, a syringe, and everyone's crowding around trying to see what she's doing, and someone shoves into her and she drops it. Crash. The thing breaks. Man, that was such a scene."

"So what happened to the kid?" Curly asked.

"What happened?" Moe asked Larry. "Do you remember?"

"They took him out of there, like to an ambulance or something. But he died."

"Shit," Curly said.

I felt relieved. At least Curly had some feeling for the kid. Maybe they'd just drop me off at Portsmouth and let me go.

"Sounds like the little bastard deserved it," he added.

"Anyway," Moe added, "I guess he had a point in being such a pain in the ass about peanuts."

"But why did he eat the chow mein, if he was always so worried?" Curly asked.

"Yeah, we all wondered about that. Maybe he was just sick of being careful. Or maybe he had . . . you know, like a death wish."

"Yeah," Curly said. "That might've been it. So how'd you capture *this* shit?"

I wasn't thrilled about the link in his thoughts.

"We didn't capture him," Moe said pleasantly. "He just wanted a ride."

"He fucked me up in there," Curly sneered. "He's gonna get more than a ride. He's gonna get a *lesson*. You know how you take a cow and burn your letter into its side?"

"It's called branding," Larry said.

"I know what it's called," Curly said. "I'm gonna brand this guy with my fist."

"I don't get it," Moe said. "I thought we were just giving him a ride."

"We're gonna kick his ass," Larry hooted, like the thought had made his night. He was one of those guys who would go along with anything, I could tell, just to belong. Jacks was like that, and he'd landed in juvenile detention three or four times, then been kicked out of school for attempted arson.

"Do we have to kick his ass?" Moe asked. "Can't we just drop him off somewhere and let him walk?"

"You don't know anything about justice," Curly said. "You know that? An eye for an eye. Ever hear that? It's from the Bible. I live by the Bible."

My mom was right. When people did something terrible, half the time they used God for a justification. My stomach turned. I was almost home, but Curly lived by the Bible.

CHAPTER 31

endemic:
commonly found in a particular country or district or group of people.

Mira's thesis about *East of Eden* was about the inability of the characters to change their nature or learn from their mistakes. There were characters who were purely evil, like Cathy, who abandons her newborn twins, shoots her husband, and then opens a brothel, or like Charles, who beats his brother, Adam, to a pulp then comes back with an axe to finish the job.

I wondered where Mira was now. Had she found another guy? Had she moved away from home like she always threatened?

The Three Stooges drove on. I prayed they were going toward Bristol. I tried again, for the millionth time in weeks, to speak, to ask the guys to let me go home. I didn't feel well. I was sick. Maybe they should let me off before they caught it.

I was shivering from the fever. It was just what Curly

needed to egg him on. Like any bully, he lived for that. A sign of fear.

"Oh, no!" Curly said. "He's shaking. The baby's scared. We don't want to hurt the baby. Pull over."

I didn't get a chance to make a run for it; Larry and Curly got a prison-guard grip on me. Moe got out of the truck, but he stood back a ways. I could tell he wasn't into it, and I was grateful to him.

The road was dark. I could hear water, like a stream, and see an embankment on the side of the road, but the only lights were in the distance. I figured if I got loose, I'd run toward those lights.

Although I knew I was in for it, it took me by surprise when Curly punched me in the stomach. "That's for stumbling into me." He punched. "That's for being a dumb shit." Another punch. "That's for fun."

The third punch brought me down. For a second, they lost their grip. Then I made my second huge mistake of the night: I didn't run.

Instead, I got to my feet, bent forward, and, like a bull, rammed into Curly. He stumbled, the second time I'd made him fall that night. Larry was on me in a second, tackling me to the ground. And now even Moe joined in, pinning my legs.

"You son of a bitch!" Curly jumped to his feet. He kicked me in the stomach and in my chest. Every time I turned, he

was there to get me. The ground was in my mouth, dirt sliding into my aching throat. I felt something shatter, like fire-
works exploding in my ribs.

"Enough." Moe let go. "You're gonna kill him."

I rolled to my side.

"One more shot." Curly pulled his leg back for another
kick and swung for my mouth, my teeth.

I couldn't lose my teeth.

That instant I remembered how Adam evades Charles
and his axe in *East of Eden*: He crawls into a ditch and hides.

With all of the energy I had left, I threw my body sideways. I felt the ground slip away as I rolled over the embankment. Then I was tumbling past bushes and branches to the
bottom.

"Jesus," Larry said. "Where the hell did he go?"

"He fell down the mountain," Moe volunteered.

"Moron," Curly sneered. "It's not a mountain. It's just a
little hill. Let's go after him."

"It's muddy," Larry argued. "These are new shoes."

I couldn't feel my body. I closed my eyes. Magical thinking. If I couldn't see them, maybe they wouldn't see me.

"Do you think he's dead?" Moe sounded worried.

"Maybe somebody gave him some peanuts in his chow
mein." Curly laughed.

"He's not dead," Larry said, but he didn't sound too
sure.

"Should we call an ambulance?" Moe's voice.

"Hell, no. And get ourselves into trouble?" Curly said.

"Let's just go," Larry suggested. "I still wanna hit Dicey's."

"I hate hanging out with you guys," Moe said. "You're such assholes. If you killed the guy, you could go to jail."

"*We,*" Curly corrected. But the word "jail" seemed to sober him. "Let's get the hell out of here."

CHAPTER 32

aftershock:
1. a quake of lesser magnitude . . . following a large earthquake in the same area. 2. a further reaction following the shock of a deeply disturbing occurrence or revelation.

When I woke up, it was still dark. Why did that keep happening? Whether I wanted it to or not. Why did I have to wake up?

I had been having a nightmare. The Three Stooges had taken me to a Laundromat, shoved me in the dryer, and then turned it on. From behind the glass door I watched the spinning world. Only it wasn't the world. It was me.

When I couldn't stand it any more, I was taken out by Cory and Bud and brought before God. He wore a long white robe, like the God in storybooks.

"You are here to be judged," God said.

"You're the one who should be judged!" I shouted. "Why do you let such terrible things happen? Why don't you do anything to help?"

"When you're God," he explained, "you know everything.

You see everything. Only you can't lift a finger. That's the sticky part. It's free will. If I didn't give it to you, none of you guys would like me."

"I don't want free will!"

"You're stuck with it." He disappeared.

I was on my back. Wet. Cold. Water lapping at my ears. My head was pounding. My skin felt glued to my face like a Halloween mask. I couldn't open one eye. Mosquitoes were landing on me, taking little nips. I didn't swat them away. *Let the mosquitoes drink and live,* I thought. *Let them take everything.*

For so long I'd been driven by the idea of going home because I somehow expected them to be there: my parents. I would return, like the time I went camping with Cory's family and his dad got us lost. We tramped around for seven hours without food, looking for the campsite, his mom shrieking at his dad the whole time, bringing up every frustration she'd ever had in life. I got back, finally, and my parents were playing cards, listening to Neil Young, drinking wine. They hadn't known about our adventure. "Our intrepid camper returns," Mom joked, giving me a big hug. I'd never been so happy to be home in my life.

I give up, I tried to say, to myself, to God who knew everything but couldn't help.

I give up.

It was what I should have done to start with.

I closed my eyes.

Up and at 'em. My mom's voice. Her hand on my forehead.

No, I told her. *I'm sleeping now. For good.*

I turned my body slowly, painfully; I laid my face in the water and willed myself to stay there. I held my own head down with my hands.

It didn't work. My body kept mutinying on me. My face kept popping up, gasping for breath.

I couldn't even get *that* right.

If I'd been at the ocean, I could have just rolled in, floated out to sea like a piece of driftwood. How many times had my dad and I done just that, floated on our surfboards aimlessly, then paddled back just before dark? To tell the truth, we liked floating and talking more than catching waves.

Rise and shine.

Mom, I can't.

You have to.

No.

Rise.

Slowly, I sat up, my ribs shrieking. I was still shivering. I couldn't feel my limbs. I leaned forward, grabbed onto the long grass, dug my fingertips into the soft earth beneath it, and crawled to the top of the embankment.

I half expected the Three Stooges to be there, boots ready to kick me back down again, but there was nothing and no one, just the lights winking down the road.

I pulled myself to my feet. My legs were working a little, even if my chest felt like a broken accordion.

For the last time, I started walking.

As I got closer to the lights, I saw that they formed a wreath. And I recognized it. It was the nursery where we bought our tomato plants in the summer, our Christmas tree in the winter. My legs moved faster, and then I was there: the main road, the 214, the sign that pointed the way: Mt. Hope Bridge. If I could reach it and get across, it was only a mile to downtown, to the red, white, and blue stripes that were painted on the road after 9/11, to the harbor, the restaurants, the shops, my shop.

CHAPTER 33

rectify:
1. to put right, to correct. 2. to purify or refine.

It was getting light when I crawled into town.

The streets were slanting. It was like this ride I once went on, where the floor drops out from under you and the walls tilt.

I was slowing down. I thought of Ms. Ross's favorite subject, again: irony. That I might die before I made it to the bookstore, or that I'd get there and it would be a deli or a real-estate office. Why should our shop still be there without us to run it?

On a weekday, many of the shopkeepers would be arriving now, their keys in one hand, cups of coffee in the other. It was a time of day I'd always loved, just this fraction of the world awake and you an intricate part of it, because you had a shop, something people needed more than anything, whether they knew it or not: books books books.

But it was Sunday; the town seemed vacant. Not a great thing for me.

I was hallucinating. I saw puddles that disappeared as soon as I reached them. My own hands kept startling me, crawling in front of me like insects.

A stronger wind came along with the light. The signs swung like blades above my head: HAL'S BARBEQUE. HAPPY FLOWERS. CORDON BLEU. The Dunkin' Donuts the town had fought.

Would I ever *walk* down this street again? Would I ever feel like I used to?

The sidewalk was cool to the touch. It was grainy and so filled with detail, like there was a world in there I'd always failed to notice. *We spend our lives looking without seeing,* I thought. *Who needs paintings when there's a sidewalk? Who needs reality when there are dreams?*

The shrill pain in my ribs returned all of a sudden. I imagined a shred of bone floating through my bloodstream.

Even if I got to the bookstore . . .

Even if it still existed, it would be locked.

Go home. Go home. The voice in my head. And only then did I think about it: that all this time the voice had been saying *home,* I'd been heading for the bookstore, not my house five blocks away.

I moved faster, my heart drumming in my chest. I reached the bicycle shop, the bank, then the dry cleaners. The smell of laundry hung in the air. I heard a car drive by, then slow, and back up. And then I saw it: our sign. Our sign still there, WALTON BOOKS, the light illuminating it like a candle at a vigil.

"Hey, kid."

I heard the car pull over and stop, the door open and close.

"Kid." Feet coming toward me.

I was almost there. When I felt his hand on my leg, I kicked out at him.

"Hey!" he said, jumping back. "I'm trying to help."

I kicked again, then crawled faster.

The man pulled something out of his pocket. I was sure it was a gun. I scrambled away, but I couldn't escape. I prepared myself for the bullet. It would rip into me.

And then I'd be fine.

The lights were on at the shop. I couldn't believe it. The door was open. Maybe it was being cleaned out, closed down. I heard the man say, "I need an ambulance. Police too. I think this guy's on drugs." And I thought, *Phone, not gun.*

"Help is coming," the man assured me, but he kept his distance.

I got to the steps. I dragged myself up them. In the store were boxes: boxes and boxes of books. And on the floor, from the entrance to the back wall, were copies of the latest Harry Potter, our best-selling books. They were lined up evenly, the exact same space between them, like stepping stones in an English garden.

Joey came into view then, moving in quick jolts as if he were being prodded by an electric wire. He stared at me a moment, lying in the entrance of the store, before he started a new row.

I heard a siren and laid my head down.

In a minute, I was surrounded by people. They were bending over me, prodding me the way the angels had.

"Joey?" I heard Margarite call, and then I could relax. I was home. I'd made it.

"Joey!" Her worried voice, but Joey was right there, I knew. Everything was fine with Joey.

"Watch out, ma'am—he's on drugs," the man with the phone said.

Margarite's scream was out of a horror movie. Under normal circumstances, it would have made me laugh.

Then she was on me. Her arms on my neck, her weight crushing my broken ribs. "Adam. Adam! I knew it was you. That you were calling me. My God. My fucking thanks be to God. Someone was spared. Everything is not gone. Everything is never fucking gone."

CHAPTER 34

coalesce:
to combine and form one whole.

I was in the hospital for six weeks. It wasn't like I needed to be in that long. My ribs healed quickly. The infection was cured. My energy returned. I got plastic surgery on a nasty wound to my head. They used diamonds to try to remove the gravel ground into my skin, but I was left with a kind of tattoo from where my face was scraped on the blacktop by the Three Stooges.

It was my lack of voice. There were neurological workups, psychiatric evaluations, a scare when an MRI showed a growth on my brain—but it ended up being a mix-up, an older man's brain scan and not mine. Poor guy.

What occurred to me, when I woke up after what felt like a month of sleep, was that I could see again. I could think straight. The timeline of my journey and my memories of the past were organized in a linear fashion rather than shooting at me randomly like missiles in some computer game.

Margarite brought in the book catalogs, the trade journals, and I pointed out what she should order, tried to communicate to her the balance between carrying the commercial stuff in quantity—Oprah's Book Club, the *New York Times* Best Sellers List—and carrying smaller quantities of the rare and the beautiful. We had loyal customers who looked to us to find stuff the chains wouldn't carry: the small presses, experimental literature, hard-to-find translations. I shook my head to show her my disapproval of books written by celebrities, even if they were on the *Times* list. My parents had been upset that celebrities with huge advances were crowding out the real writers, people who had devoted their lives to their craft. But I wanted Margarite to add her energy to the store, to pick stuff she liked.

She wanted more kids' books. She added a section on disabilities, then sent out fliers to schools and gave talks on the subject. She started a Friday night reading series for local writers.

Cory visited me once. He kept blinking his eyes. "Shit, Adam. I don't know what to say. Shit." Finally, he came over and hugged me. "I'm just glad you're alive, man. Just so glad." Ms. Ross came, too. She didn't say much, just squeezed my hand and gave me a look like, *Goddamn it, you are going to be fine, even if I have to drag you to the ends of the earth.*

Then there was Mira. Her first response to me was the opposite of Margarite's. She walked into the hospital room and stared at me, just stared, like she was seeing a new country for the first time. Her eyes got wide; her voice was as silent as mine.

Finally, she came closer and put out a single finger to touch me. It was as if she thought I might crumble into pieces, or disappear like a ghost. As soon as she touched me, I started sobbing. For the first time since the accident, I cried. And she joined me—a regular crying fest.

She came every day. She showed me cards from the other kids, and she read to me. She read *Oliver Twist,* then started on *Huck Finn.* It kind of cracked me up that she brought in books about young boys.

When the nurse wasn't around, she climbed into bed with me. The first time she did that, I remembered, with a stab of guilt, Stacey, my Wiccan friend—my desertion of her, and worse, my unfaithfulness to Mira.

Mira was always a mind reader, though. One day she looked me straight in the eye and said, "Anything that happened when you were away—anything—is history. It doesn't matter now. It doesn't count. Because you're back. Understand?"

I nodded.

"And you're gonna talk. I know that. You'll talk when you're ready."

Yeah. I knew that too. I just had to get rid of the tears that were crowding my throat, to make space for my voice to rise. I worked on that, on the crying. I worked on it every day.

In addition to seeing the past with clarity, I could also envision the future. I could see myself walking to collect my diploma. The school would forgive me the time I'd missed, and I'd graduate with my class. I'd go to Brown, like I planned. I wouldn't live in the dorms with the other kids, though. I'd stay in Bristol with Margarite and Joey and run the bookstore. Mira would go to Johnson and Wales, so she could be a chef. We'd make the drive to Providence together.

I could see the headstone I would put on my parents' graves, one headstone for the two of them, with my Dad's poem inscribed on it. *Still the wing flaps. The feathers lift. On air as bold as strong.*

They were in the historic cemetery by my house. I would go there every week for the rest of my life and talk to them about books, the shop, Margarite, Joey, Mira, and the grandkids that would eventually come.

People don't die. That isn't how it happens. They float inside of you. Like leaves on water. They drift away sometimes, pulled under by the current, tugged toward the shore. But then they resurface, defining you as much by their absence as they did when they were there.